IN LOVE WITH AN OUTLAW

REIGN

In Love With An Outlaw

REIGN

© 2022

Published by *Reign Presents*

All rights reserved.

This is a work of fiction.

Names, characters, businesses, places, events, and incidents are either the products of the author's imagination or used in a fictitious manner.

Any resemblance to actual persons, living or dead, or actual events is purely coincidental.

No part of this book may be reproduced, stored in or introduced into a retrieval system, or transmitted, in any form, or by any means (electronic, mechanical, photocopying, recording, or otherwise), without prior written consent from both the author and publisher except brief quotes used in reviews. The scanning, uploading, and distribution of this book via the internet or any other means without permission is illegal and punishable by law.

CONTENTS

Special Thanks	v
Prologue	1
1. Blaze	5
2. Laila	17
3. Blaze	27
4. Deontre	37
5. Blaze	43
6. Laila	47
7. Blaze	53
8. Laila	61
9. Deontre	69
10. Angel	73
11. Blaze	75
12. Deontre	81
13. Blaze	85
14. Deontre	91
15. Angel	95
16. Laila	99
17. Laila	103
18. Blaze	109
19. Deontre	117
20. Blaze	121
21. Deontre	125
22. Blaze	137
23. Deontre	145
24. Blaze	149
25. Roxy	153
26. Black	159
27. Angel	161
28. Laila	163

29. Roxy	169
30. Blaze	173
31. Laila	175
32. Roxy	181
1	187
2	193
Connect with Reign	199

SPECIAL THANKS

First, I have to thank my creator for the gift of expression. I can honestly say I never saw it coming that I would become a published author and be able to turn my passion into a paycheck.

I want to thank my readers, supporters, and followers. I write as a stress release, but I also write for y'all. For those who have been with me from the beginning, I thank you for your loyalty and patience as I start completely over to revamp and rebrand myself again! For those who are just getting to know me, welcome. I have a lot of stories to tell and a lot of experiences to share. I promise you won't be disappointed!

To Mehki, you are my inspiration... my motivation... my reason for being. I love you, son.

PROLOGUE

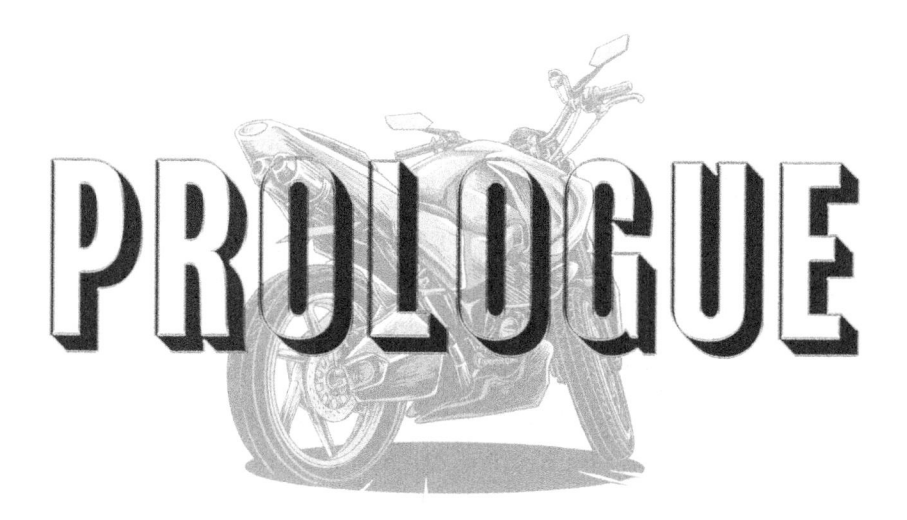

Blaze slowly dismounted from her motorcycle and strutted across the parking lot into the grocery store. She realized the day before that she had forgotten to grab a few things she needed, so even though she was already running late, she had no choice but to make the stop. Grabbing a cart, she went through the list she made in her head: paper plates, solo cups, napkins, and cutlery. Blaze started filling the cart with the items so she could attempt to get in and out as quickly as possible. She needed one last pack of paper plates that was just out of her reach on the top shelf. She stood on her tiptoes to try to reach it and *boom!* A charm from her unique Pandora bracelet must have gotten caught on a piece of plastic on the surrounding products because she accidently pulled everything in front of her off the shelf and onto the floor.

"Let me help you with that," said a particularly smooth voice from behind her. Blaze turned around to see a tall, sexy, brown-skinned man with a clean cut and perfect smile appear out of nowhere.

"Thanks, but I got it," Blaze responded with an attitude

while trying her best to act uninterested with his presence. Based on the overly sultry tone of his voice, he was clearly interested with more than helping her clean the mess, and she didn't have the time to entertain him. She had things to do, and she knew she didn't have time for the meaningless conversation that was sure to follow.

"I'm sure you do... but I'm still here to help," he replied with a handsome smirk. He began to pick up some of the paper towels and cups she pulled to the floor in her haste.

"Since you insist on helping, can you grab that pack of plates up there for me?" she asked him. When the man reached up, Blaze's instincts caused her scan his body with her eyes and check for tattoos first to see if he was affiliated with a gang. He had no tattoos that she could see, and he was clean cut... had clean clothes with creases in them. *This nigga must have some type of boring corporate job, and he's definitely not from here*, she thought.

"I think we got up all of the mess you made," the man told her jokingly.

"Funny... but thanks for grabbing that for me. I appreciate it umm... I'm sorry. What's your name?" she asked.

"Deontre... but everyone calls me Trey... and you are?"

"Blaze," she answered while checking him out a bit better.

"Blaze, how about I give you my number, and if you ever need help cleaning up another one of your messes, you can give me a call."

"Mmm hmm, real cute," she replied, slightly amused. Blaze took out her phone to save Trey's number.

"It was a pleasure to meet you, Mr. Deo—sorry, Trey. You'll be hearing from me," Blaze said, sweetening up her voice a little. She usually never gave out her number to men she randomly ran into, but there was something about this one, and the attraction between the two was inevitable.

"It was a pleasure meeting you, too, Ms. Blaze. I'll be waiting anxiously on that call," he said while flashing his perfect smile at her.

"Soon, I hope," he added on as she walked away from him.

When Blaze left the store, she looked back to see Trey looking her up and down from the checkout line. *He's fine and everything, but I probably won't even call. Outta town ass nigga just trying to find a lil' bust down to occupy him while he's here. He got the wrong fuckin' one*, Blaze thought while smiling and waving at him.

CHAPTER 1
BLAZE

"CHANGE IS THE LAW OF LIFE."

"Aye, yo!" Blaze answered her cell phone half annoyed. The thick Texas summer heat mixed with her twenty-two-inch weave and her leather vest put her in a sour mood by default. She was ready to get in some air conditioning or hop on her Kawasaki Ninja 300 and dip in and out of traffic, feeling the wind whip through her hair.

"Where the hell are you?" an angry voice replied from the other end of her phone. It was her best friend, Laila, of course. No one else could get away with speaking to Blaze in that tone.

"You know the cookout started at five! How is it that the boss lady gon' be late? You can't be the MC President, operating on CP time," Laila said. Blaze laughed a little, being that most of the time, she was the one who was late.

"Alright! Chill, trick. I'm on the road now. I'll be there in fifteen," Blaze said. She and Laila had been best friends since they were children, so she never took it personally when she was on the receiving end of Laila's attitude. It was just her personality.

Blaze was sure Laila's attitude would be wiped clean when her crew saw the reason she was late. Today was the annual Summer Kick-Off Cook-Out for her motorcycle club, the Nubian Riders. Weeks ago, she ordered new vests for everyone because the ones they were currently wearing had been through hell and back, to say the least. Blaze had gone to the store to pick up extra supplies for the cookout when she had gotten the call that the vests were ready to be picked up. She had to go home and trade her motorcycle in for the truck she drove from time to time so she could bring the vests to the cookout.

Pulling up to her bar, Blaze was greeted by the smell of barbecue and the sight of her best friend waiting on her out front smoking a blunt.

"Finally! The HBIC has arrived! You had me waiting on you in this hot ass sun. I mean, Black people burn, too, but your light-skinned ass wouldn't know about that," Laila said while hugging Blaze and laughing.

"Forget that shit you're talking. Pass me that there you're smoking on and go to the back of the truck while you check allllll that mothafuckin' attitude that's been in your voice," Blaze said. Laila gave Blaze a hard side-eye as she took her instructions, handed her friend the blunt, and walked to the back of the truck to see the stacks of biker vests wrapped in plastic.

"Hell yeah! I'm not mad anymore!" Laila almost shouted while jumping on to the bed of the truck to find her own vest.

"I put something special on yours too, babe. Check your collar," Blaze said while winking. Laila found the vest with her name on it and looked at the collar. Blaze had a tiny pair of boxing gloves sewn on to the vest for her best friend.

Laila wasn't actually Laila's real name. It was her club nickname. She was the fighter in the group. Every time the girls went out of town, and sometimes at their own bar as well, she would get them into some type of trouble and would end up fighting, so Blaze started calling her Laila, like Laila Ali the boxer.

"It's perfect... describes me to a 'T'. Thanks, girl."

Laila held the vest out in front of her admiring the new look. She was about to take off the one she was currently wearing to put on the new one when Blaze stopped her.

"Aht aht! Not yet, bitch! We're all switching out at the same time. Plus, Angel gets her vest today. She won't be a prospect anymore, so you have to at least be cordial now," Blaze told her in a raspy almost inaudible voice while expelling smoke from her lungs. Laila rolled her eyes at Blaze.

"I still can't believe you let the white girl in... or whatever the fuck she is. Something is not right about that chick. It's like she's trying too hard to fit in or to prove herself... I don't really know, but if she didn't want to stick out like a sore thumb, she shouldn't have started rolling with a group of all Black female motorcycle riders," Laila let out with contempt hanging from every word.

"Mostly Black, trick! She's mixed, not white, and I let in the smart-mouthed troublemaker who's always showing her ass, so why not let the *white* girl in?" Blaze asked while pulling Laila's ponytail that hung all the way to the top of her butt.

"When are you going to cut this fake ass shit anyway?" Blaze asked with giggle and an extra hard yank of her best friend's hair.

"Cut your own shit, bitch. I ain't cutting my hair. This ain't weave with your low-key hatin' ass!" Laila shot back while playfully swatting her friend's hand away.

"I swear you were raised by got-damned sailors. You're always fucking cursing!" Blaze said. She paused and looked at Laila with a smirk, and they both burst out laughing.

Blaze and Laila grabbed the vests and headed to the back side of the club where everyone else was outside.

"Aye, yo! The party is here!" Blaze shouted, and a chorus of yells and cat calls greeted her. She held get-togethers for her girls often, but there was nothing like the Summer Kick-Off. Everyone came out, including the club members' families, regulars that partied at the club, and members of their brother organization, the Kings.

Laila and Blaze set the vests on one of the patio tables as everyone gathered around.

"Everybody, listen up!" Blaze yelled to the large crowd. She jumped on top of the nearest table to stand so everyone could see and hear her, although her beauty and commanding presence already made her stand out everywhere.

"I just want to thank everyone for coming out today. We're going to have a good time and get stuffed on some great food, like always. Roxy, over here, is going to do games with the kids while the food is cooking," Blaze announced as she gestured in the direction of one of her club members in the back of the crowd. A tall slim caramel-colored young woman raised her hand near the back of the crowd to wave to everyone.

"Right now, I do have a surprise for all the club members. You all saw me and Laila come in with bundles wrapped in plastic, and I know you're wondering what's going on. Well, our new vests finally came in, and everyone gets theirs today!"

Blaze looked through the crowd and immediately spotted Angel, whose slightly tinted vanilla skin easily stood out in a vast sea of brown.

"Angel, come up here!" Blaze shouted, and everyone whistled

and clapped. Blaze jumped down from the table to stand beside Angel once she walked up.

"Angel has been with us for a little while now. She's become an asset to the club in too many ways to count and has proven her loyalty time and time again. We may get a lot of criticism for bringing something *different* to the group, but Angel is our sister no matter what, so if they have a problem with her, they have a problem with me!" People in the crowd clapped and cheered a bit as Blaze wrapped her arm around Angel's shoulders. Laila cut her eyes at Blaze as she grabbed Angel's vest from the top of the stack.

"Welcome to the Nubian Riders, baby!" Blaze yelled. Everyone at the cookout went crazy as Blaze helped Angel put on her vest for the first time and hugged her hard.

"The rest of you ladies can come on and switch out. Just leave your old vest on this table to the left of us. We can cut and switch over the patches later," she told them. Blaze skimmed through the crowd she noticed Laila disappeared into. She spotted her best friend walking away from the crowd and into the building that housed her club-like bar. Blaze grabbed Laila's vest and ran to catch up to her.

Blaze finally caught up with Laila inside the club. Laila was already behind the bar, pouring herself shots.

"You better slow down on that shit. The kids are here until nine, so we don't need you turning up and fighting before then. We really don't need you turning up and fighting at all, but you wouldn't be you if you didn't. What's your problem today, anyway? You've got more attitude than usual," Blaze mentioned as she watched Laila down a second shot.

"I just don't agree with your decision. That's all. You're in charge. What you say goes, of course, but if you want me to be cordial to that little girl, then you better let me have these shots. My patience is pretty damn thin when I'm completely sober. You of all people should know that," Laila shot back as she laughed and poured a third shot.

"Oh... you have patience? Congratulations, bitch! When that happen?" Blaze asked as they them laughed.

"But for real, why do you hate that girl so much? You don't even know enough about her to hate her. From the day she stepped to us, you haven't really fooled with her. What's the deal with y'all? Some secret beef I don't know about?" Blaze asked.

"Do you ever get a feeling...? About anything, I mean... just a feeling that something isn't right? That shit is real. You don't imagine those feelings. When my mom was alive, she used to tell me all about vibrations..." Laila said as she downed that third shot.

"....and energies and shit like that," she continued. Blaze opened her mouth in protest of her best friend taking a fourth shot, but Laila quickly cut her off before she could get her words out.

"That was the last one!" Laila said while laughing and capping the bottle of cheap brown liquor.

"But yeah, like I was saying, all people, places, and things have vibrations. You know? Some are good, and some are bad. When you get a bad feeling about going somewhere or that something isn't right about a person, then you have to pay attention to that feeling because that shit is real. Your gut knows. They call it your second brain or some shit like that."

Laila let out a long breath while putting the bottle back under the counter in her secret spot.

"Here you go with all that mystic spirituality bullshit," Blaze said while dramatically rolling her eyes.

"You better do your research on your ancestors, baby girl. You may be light skinned, but you're just as Black as me on the inside."

"Okay, I'm not in the mood to debate religion, God, or creation with you today. That's that cheap ass liquor talking. Come on. We're about to get our meeting out of the way and handle the business while the food is cooking and before everybody gets to drinking and all that," Blaze stated. Blaze handed Laila her new vest to put on.

"Mark my words, honey. You're going to regret bringing Angel into this club and into the business, but what you say goes, so I guess I don't have a choice but to deal with it. Right?"

"Bingo, bitch!" Blaze said while laughing, giving Laila's ponytail another tug, and helping her with her new vest. The two of them walked out the back door and went to find each member amongst the crowd to bring them inside for the club meeting. The ladies went inside the club, following Blaze to the back office where they would have complete privacy.

"Make sure it's shut all the way," Laila said to Angel with an attitude, as Angel was the last one through the door.

"Alright, everybody. We need to make this quick so we can get back to the fam." Blaze started off with a serious look on her face.

"Angel is a member now, and I don't give a damn who has a problem with it. She's put in the work time and time again, and we're going to need all the help we can get going forward. Business is about to step up because new opportunities have presented themselves," Blaze added. There was nervous mumbling among the group.

"As of last month, we stopped the large movement of the greenery," Blaze told them.

"That's weed, in case you didn't know, *newbie*... wit'cho *green* ass," Laila whispered in Angel's ear while smirking. Blaze shot Laila a look that said she better chill the fuck out. Angel cut her eyes at Laila as Blaze continued.

"The risk was far greater than the reward, even with the amount of weight we were moving. What we're about to do is up our pill weight and take on something new, moving some fire power. Before any of you say anything, don't worry. We'll be getting help from our brothers, the Kings," Blaze added. A few of the ladies started whistling and cat calling.

"Cut the shit, ladies! This is gon' be strictly business!" Laila said aloud.

"She's right. This is strictly about money. I'm dead ass serious. Prove yourself in this game first. Get your pussy wet later. Roxy does an amazing job with the bike customizing, but let's be real... business is only booming around tax time, the beginning of the summer, and right before Black Bike Week. The bar opens almost every night, but alcohol sales are not about to pay all our bills. Plus, my father is getting older, and he won't be running the Kings forever. We have to learn the business fast and hold our own out here if we want to hold on to our main source of income."

"Who you calling old?" asked a commanding voice from the door.

"Well... speak of the devil," Blaze said while weaving her way through the ladies and toward that voice. It was her father, Anthony, who most people called Ant for short, which was quite ironic due to his large stature. His club name in the Kings used to be Hulk, due to the fact he had body builder sized muscles and practically turned into a monster when someone crossed him and made him angry, but he had long since let that nickname go.

"You ladies continue. Just act like I'm not even here," Anthony told them. He nodded in Blaze's direction for her to keep going.

"We have a delivery that needs to be made in one week, just pills this time. Y'all know the deal," Blaze said. Three of the members raised their hands, including Angel. Laila looked at Angel's hand and immediately raised hers as well.

"You ladies be here tomorrow before the club opens to the public so that we can go over the details. That's all for now. Go eat. Remember, all the kiddos need to be gone from here tonight by nine at the absolute latest, and the bar opens at ten to the public. After that, you're free to get fucked up 'til your heart's content. Meeting adjourned!" Blaze yelled as she slammed her hand down on the table. Anthony shook his head while laughing. All the ladies filed out of the back office until it was just Blaze and her father left alone.

"You seem to be handling things like a boss, as always. How did they react to knowing y'all are going to start moving guns too?" Blaze's father asked.

"Some of them seem to be hesitant, but I think we'll be okay as a whole. It's just something they're not used to. It comes with different risks and a different type of clientele. We'll get it done regardless, even if I have to move it all myself. You know how I do, Pops," she told him as they dapped each other up with a laugh.

"Good. I really came back here for another reason. I was just letting you know that some of the Kings were planning on coming to the club to party tonight once all the kids are gone, and I know how you feel about them on a personal level. I heard

Black was coming too," Anthony added. He looked at his daughter, trying to read her face for a reaction. Black was the Vice President of the Kings, and also the ex-fiancé of Blaze.

"I'm cool. I'm not stuntin' Black, and as long as they don't bring any drama into my bar, then it's fine for them to be here. It's Laila they need to be worried about. If she sees any of their ol' ladies disrespected in front of her, that's going to be a problem they don't want to deal with," she said. Blaze laughed to herself while picturing her best friend whooping a grown man's ass, which she had done many times before.

"Are you partying with us tonight, old man? It might keep away trouble if they see the big boss man in the building."

"We both know you're more than capable of handling trouble if need be," Anthony told her with a wink and a chuckle.

"Your name carries respect, just like mine does these days, baby girl. Carry yourself accordingly. I'll leave the next generation to have their own fun tonight," he told her, and with that, they went back to join the cookout. As soon as Blaze stepped out the door, Laila grabbed her by the arm and pulled her to the side of the building.

"Really, Blaze?

What's your problem now?"

"She's fresh out of the gate, and she's already going on a run… our first weapon run at that!" Laila all but shouted. Blaze rolled her eyes and looked around to make sure no one was close enough to hear them.

"Look. I've let you talk shit just between the two of us about my decision to let Angel in, but don't forget that even though we may be best friends, I'm still your president. Let's separate business from personal for a minute. What I say goes, so suck that shit up. I'm not going to do anything that would hurt any of my girls, especially you. I would think you would have a lil' more trust in me by now... as long as we've known each other. I'm just trying to make sure we're all eating good in the future. Oh, and if you try to embarrass her in the middle of a meeting again, I'm going to embarrass yo' ass!" Blaze told her with authority.

"Damn, Blaze! It's like that? You're really going to boss up on me like that over this new bitch?" Laila asked, shocked.

"Check all that. This is business. You know you're my right hand," Blaze said truthfully. Even though Blaze could tell Laila clearly wasn't able to separate the business from the personal as well as she did, she couldn't dwell on it at the moment. Blaze rejoined the crowd, leaving Laila standing there, still salty.

CHAPTER 2
LAILA

"KEEP CALM AND... PARTY!"

It was close to midnight, and the bar was pumping. Everyone's family members were long gone, and it was time to have some real fun. Laila was in the back of the bar in their locker room checking out her outfit before she joined everyone. She eyed her black Polo boots, her short shorts, and her cut off tank top, an outfit that displayed the tattoos that practically covered her body.

"Damn. You look good, mama," Laila said aloud to herself while double checking her edges were laid. She had to make sure her signature ponytail was on point.

"Glad to see I wasn't imagining you're a crazy self-centered bitch," said a voice from behind her. Laila whipped around and saw Angel leaning against the door. Her appearance had changed since the cookout too. She was wearing a mini skirt and a sleeveless top with boots similar to Laila's. She was also wearing her new club vest.

"You better be glad I've been drinking already, or I might have chin checked your ass just because," Laila said while turning back toward the mirror. Angel laughed at Laila's idle words.

"You know... you threaten me so much it doesn't even faze me anymore. I think you just like to hear yourself talk sometimes," Angel said back. Laila ignored Angel's comment and continued to verbally take jabs at her.

"Do you ride in that skirt? Because you know that's beyond hoeish, right? We're riders, not someone's ol' lady or a pass-around. We're bosses, so you need to look the part," Laila reminded her while glancing over her shoulder at Angel's mini skirt.

"I've got on spanks. Chill. And besides, if I wanted to show *it* off, it's pretty enough for the world to see," Angel said, softly patting the front of her skirt where her pussy print would be. The comeback actually made Laila smirk, but she didn't let Angel see it. Laila put on her vest, turned sideways to see how her ass looked in her shorts, and then walked toward Angel, standing a few inches from her face.

"Let's get something straight. Blaze may accept you, but I'll still be watching yo' ass because I don't trust yo' ass. This isn't a black and white thing either. This is a real recognize real and you looking real unfamiliar kind of thing. I'm being nice to you out of respect, but watch yourself *Becky*," Laila said while flicking a piece of Angel's obnoxious blonde and dark brown streaked curly hair.

"I'm not even white, racist bitch."

Laila shook her head and snickered at the statement.

"Close e-fucking-nough. Oh, and watch that pretty lil' mouth of yours. I ain't gon' be too many more bitches. Mmm kay?"

Laila aggressively brushed Angel's shoulder with her own as she headed toward the door, leaving Angel standing there with a stank look on her face. When Laila walked out of the changing room, she almost immediately ran into Blaze.

"Ayyye! Go best friend! That's my best friend! That's my best friend," Laila sang when she saw Blaze, and for good reason. As the president, Blaze always made sure she looked her best when she stepped out, and even more so when she was at her own bar. That night, she was blacked out from head to toe; black Polo boots that matched Laila's, some black designer jeans with frayed slits covering the thighs, and a black and white Moschino bra top under her vest. All twenty-two inches of her bone straight Brazilian hair was hanging.

"You're a trip!" Blaze said, laughing as Laila tried to twerk on her.

"You're looking bad as hell too," she added, slapping Laila on the ass.

"Everybody is tonight. Hey, did my pops tell you some of the Kings would be here tonight?" Blaze asked skeptically.

"Mmm hmm. I heard a certain someone is going to be here too. That's probably why you're looking extra sexy tonight, on the low," Laila said as Blaze gave her a side eye.

But nah, I'm good as long as they don't come in here on no bullshit. Real talk, Blaze. They forget we run things over this way. Our politics aren't the same as theirs when it comes to how a woman is supposed to be treated."

"Don't I know it! I won't even tell you to behave because this is Summer Kick-Off night. There's no telling who is out there, and I know you. Let's get some drinks. I need to catch up with you," Blaze said. She grabbed Laila's hand and turned to join the party.

As soon as the girls got down the hall and through the door, the volume of the music was amplified. The DJ was beginning his spin of twerk music to try to get the party started. Blaze's bar was not normally a place to dance but mainly drink, play pool, eat, and smoke in piece. Big events completely changed the atmosphere.

Laila and Blaze sat down at the bar and motioned for Roxy, who skipped everyone else who was gesturing for a drink and came straight to them. Roxy was definitely a little different from the other girls. Although she wasn't significantly older than the rest of the girls, she was still the mother of the gang. Roxy had gotten all the partying out of her system a long time ago, so most of time she volunteered to work the bar and keep an eye on all the other girls while they got turnt up.

"Y'all looking sexy tonight, as usual," Roxy said as she walked over.

"Thanks, love," Blaze replied.

"You're looking gorgeous too, honey," Laila added. When Roxy worked the bar, she didn't feel the need to get dolled up, but she had a very natural beauty about herself, regardless of whether she chose to flaunt it or not. Her caramel-colored skin was flawless, and her long full eyelashes complemented her hazel eyes. Not to mention, she was tall, which usually brought attention to her immediately, no matter her appearance.

"Guess what?" Blaze asked while baiting them with a sly grin.

"I'll bite... what's up?" Roxy asked while leaning closer.

"So..." Blaze started while looking back and forth between her two friends.

"I met the fine ass dude inside the grocery store earlier today."

"So, that's the real reason you were late, ol' fast ass!" Laila said while nudging Blaze's arm.

"Cut that! I'm not you, trick. Nothing happened. We didn't even end up talking long. I just met him. I knocked over a bunch of stuff in the grocery store while I was rushing to get here, and he stopped to help me. We flirted a little, I guess, but I didn't think anything of it. He ended up giving me his number," Blaze said with a little excitement in her eyes. Roxy smiled and slapped her hand on the bar.

"Well, damn. Who taught you how to flirt again? I'm joking, but finally! I was starting to worry you would never move on from that asshole, Black," Roxy added.

"Yeah, and Laila, you're always talking about your gut feelings and vibrations and all that. Well... if I did believe in that stuff, then I would have to say that he felt right," Blaze told her.

"Well, damn. This dude must be *fine* fine to have you talking like that. You better call him, or I will. I know that pussy got cobwebs on it by now," Laila said jokingly.

"Shut up! Don't worry about this kitty. I don't need no man to make sure *she* straight. I might have a girlfriend for all you know."

"Yeah. Imagine that," Laila commented with a laugh.

"Whatever! He's definitely fine, though. I think I'll call him but not because of how he looks. I'm not you, Laila." Blaze laughed.

"Damn. Look who's coming over here," Laila spat while her whole tone did a one eighty. Angel was walking toward the ladies to join in on the conversation. If looks could kill, Angel would have dropped dead right then because Laila was staring daggers through the girl.

"Behave!" Blaze said while looking Laila straight in her eyes. Laila gave Blaze a fake smile and turned back toward the new girl approaching.

"What are y'all drinking?" Angel asked with a chipper expression when she walked up.

"I'm about to handle that right now, actually. What can I get for my sisters tonight?" Roxy asked while looking Angel up and down.

"Crown and Coke for me," Blaze said.

"Hen-dawg for me, baby girl... Hennessey, straight up!" Laila answered, surveying the bar and taking in her surroundings.

"Of course. What about you, newbie?" Roxy asked.

"Umm... just Cîroc and Sprite, I guess," Angel said. Laila whipped around with her attention locked on Angel

"Hell no! If it ain't brown, don't bring it around. Roxy, bring her ass some Crown Apple and Coke. That girl talking about *I guess*. Bitch, do you even drink? Who doesn't know their own drink of choice? Damn. Suspect as fuck," Laila said, cutting in and speaking directly to Angel.

"Let that girl order what hell she wants! Damn! You always O.D.," Blaze said while giving Laila a look that was an entire conversation in itself.

"It's cool, Blaze. I'll take Crown Apple and Coke," Angel said to Roxy before she shot Laila a knowing look.

"So, Laila, I thought everyone only used nicknames in here. Why don't you?" Angel asked while turning to Laila.

"Oh, Laila isn't my real name. That *is* my nickname. It's short for Laila Ali because I whoop ass... often... and very well... so remember that," Laila replied with a smirk.

"Noted," Angel shot back with an equally bitchy smirk and an eye roll.

"What about you?" Angel continued as Roxy returned with their drinks.

"What *about* me?" Roxy questioned while leaning against the bar and sizing the new girl up again.

"How did you get the name Roxy?" she asked. Blaze and Laila

glanced at one another when Angel asked the question and then looked at Roxy.

"It's okay, Blaze... Laila... I don't mind telling the story, because I'm not that girl anymore, and she's one of our sisters now. Some years ago, I was living out in the country, and I was lost. Not literally, but you know... I was just doing everything wrong. I was poisoning my mind and my body... drunk and high all the damn time. Well, the Nubian Riders happened to stop through a bar I frequented, and this night in particular was a rough one for me. I just lost my two kids to DSS that morning, so I was waist deep in my own pity party and shit, trying to numb the pain like most addicts do. Long story short... Blaze here found me passed out behind that bar, brought me to a hospital here, and I just never left. My most common drug of choice at the time, roxi, turned into my nickname. It's not too deep. Nicknames never are around here," Roxy said with a smile and winked at Angel before walking off to tend to the other customers.

"Yeah, and now she's all spiritual... connected to the motherland and our ancestors and what not. Personally, I'm with it!" Laila added in.

"Boss lady, I didn't forget about you. The tale behind your name has to be, by far, the most interesting. Tell me a story," Angel said while leaning closer to Blaze.

"I'll tell all of you a story if I get to tuck all you beautiful ladies in bed afterward!" said a familiar voice. Both Laila and Blaze whipped around to see that Black walked up. He tried to put his arm around Laila's shoulders while eyeing Blaze and checking her out from head to toe, but Laila shrugged him off her and punched him in the shoulder.

"Hot damn, slugger! I was just coming over to speak. I'm not trying to start no problems. You must be half past drunk as fuck already, Laila," Black said while laughing. Laila's punch hadn't fazed him due to his size. Most people said he was the son that Anthony never had because physically, they were built the exact same way, muscles and all.

"What the hell do you want, Black? It's bad enough that you and your boys are even here," Blaze said in a bitter tone.

"The Kings couldn't miss the Summer Kick-Off after party, now, could we?" he replied. Leaning down to speak directly into Blaze's ear, he continued.

"We're about to start working together, so you have to be nice to me, Egypt."

Hovering near her ear, allowing his breath to tickle her lobe, Black reached down and forcefully grabbed a handful of Blaze's ass, causing her to snap. For some reason, the disrespect of the ass grab, coupled with hearing Black say her real name set Blaze off.

"My name is Blaze, mothafucka!" she shouted. Blaze elbowed Black to get him off her.

"Stupid bitch!" Black yelled while groaning, doubling over, and clutching his ribs. Blaze caught Black off guard and used all her strength, so he really felt that pain.

"Watch who you call a bitch!" Laila yelled as she threw her drink in Black's face and kneed him in the nuts while he was distracted. That kick brought him all the way down to his knees. Blaze took off, visibly upset, to the office in the back of the club. Laila walked behind the bar, grabbed a bottle, and broke it against the edge of the bar. She walked back over to Black who was still on his knees holding his jewels, and he was now surrounded by a few other members of the Kings.

"If you ever put your hands on her again, I will shove this broken bottle so far up your ass, you'll shit glass for a year!" Laila said into his ear. She sat back down at the bar, knowing she would probably pay for humiliating Black one way or another.

CHAPTER 3
BLAZE

"THINKING 'HERE GOES NOTHING' COULD BE THE START OF EVERYTHING."

The next morning, Blaze woke up in the changing room of the club. After the run-in she and Laila had with Black the night before, the two ladies stayed in the back of the club drinking and talking shit about Black until they passed out. As Blaze got up from the sofa to go freshen up, she grabbed her phone to check her messages. She scrolled through the contacts and happened upon Trey's name. It was early, so if she called, he probably wouldn't answer. Thinking on it, Blaze didn't even actually want him to answer. She preferred to leave a message so he could call back. It would make it feel like he was pursuing her instead of the other way around.

When she pressed the telephone symbol by Trey's name, the call connected almost immediately, and the conversation timer started. *Shit*, she thought.

"This Trey. What the lick read?" he asked. Blaze suppressed a laugh at hearing the way Trey answered the phone.

"What the lick read? What the hell? Umm... how old are you again?" Blaze responded.

"Ahhh, this must be the beautiful, eye captivating Blaze that

I met yesterday afternoon. I'm glad you called. How are you this morning?" he said smoothly.

"How did you know it was me?"

"I recognized your voice, miss lady... and I also don't give out my number like that. I don't have a lot of women calling me," he answered.

"You don't have a lot calling you, which means there are *some* calling you," Blaze replied while softening up her voice a little.

"How funny, but no. I'm one hundred percent single. I don't have any boo's, buddies, or ex's that think they're still my boo, baby mamas, or a secret wife somewhere. Based on the fact that you actually called, I'm going to assume you're single, too."

"This time, your assumption is right. I'm single," she stated, agreeing with him.

"Since we got that out the way, I want to cut straight to the point... You're going out with me," Trey declared as opposed to actually asking her.

"I like how you're sort of telling me instead of actually asking me. I'll tell you now... one thing you should know is that I'm grown. If we go out, we're going *out*. I don't want to go the club or a bar because I own one. That doesn't excite me. I don't want to just go to dinner and a movie, and I don't want to just *chill*. I haven't been on a date in a long time, so don't make me regret saying yes. You'll see for yourself that I have extremely high standards, so I'm going to need you to get creative," Blaze articulated to him.

"A woman who knows what she wants... I like that. Don't worry about the destination. Just bring you and those gorgeous eyes. I'll handle the rest," Trey replied. Blaze couldn't tell if Trey was being genuine or running game, but either way, he had her grinning like a teenage girl talking to her crush.

"How about tonight?" Trey asked.

"I can't go tonight. I have work to do. What about tomorrow night?" Blaze replied.

"I have to check the weather, but tomorrow night should be perfect," Trey said. Blaze figured that was an odd response, but she paid it no mind.

"I'll see you then, sir," she told him.

"Looking forward to it, ma'am," Trey replied, and with that, they both hung up.

"Who are you talking to this early with that lame ass kitten voice?"

Blaze turned around to see her best friend, Laila, sitting up on her own pallet, rubbing her forehead.

"It was just that guy I was telling you and Roxy about last night. His name is Deontre... Trey," Blaze answered.

"You'll probably have to tell me all about him again later because I don't remember half the shit that happened last night. Right now... I need an Ibuprofen and another shot," Laila said as she got up and walked toward the hall to head to the bar.

"I really need to stop drinking so gahdamn much," Laila told Blaze in a groggy voice.

"Yeah. You do. You came at Black real hard. You know my dad is going to have something to say about that, right?"

"Yeah. If he's the man I know he is, he'll dap me up for handling Black after he disrespected you like that, feeling you up like that in *your* own bar like you're some pass-around. Real talk, though, we both should probably watch our backs around Black from now on. He's not going to let that go because we embarrassed him in front of almost half his crew," Laila said with a little worry in her tone. Waking up on a soberer side of the spectrum this morning allowed her to digest the seriousness of what happened the night before.

"I'm not going to think twice about Black. Fuck him. I can handle myself just fine when it comes to him," Blaze replied. The encounter between herself, Laila, and Black flashed across her mind, and she quickly brushed it off.

"Call the prospects in today. They need to clean this place up. We have that meeting tonight and probably the gun drop right after that. The Kings aren't my problem. Whatever they decide to do after business is done is cool, but I don't want my girls driving all the way back home after they've been up all night. Y'all will be staying here to wind down afterward... and yes. Before you even say anything, Angel will be here too," I told her. Laila closed her eyes and shook her head.

"I ain't even got the energy to—"

"Make sure the girls know what they're supposed to wear and all that. The bikes need to be gassed up and checked, and... I think that's all," Blaze told Laila, cutting her off and trying to think if she left anything out.

"Yes, Mommy. We'll make sure we don't forget our lunch boxes and juice too... and to look both ways before we cross the street," Laila said in a baby-like voice while poking fun at Blaze.

"Alright. Keep on!" Blaze said.

"Just do what I say. We have to get this first run done right so that my dad knows we can handle it. We need to get to this money. Almost all these women have families to feed, and they're depending on us to get this shit right."

THE NEXT DAY

Blaze was home, getting ready for her date that was that afternoon. She had no idea what Trey had planned for the two of them, and to be honest, she was a bit excited and slightly nervous.

Blaze walked over to her closet and just stood there. A wave of anxiety fell over her at that moment. She was the leader of the Nubian Riders, so by nature she had a tough exterior. To most, she came off as hard core, but underneath it all, she was truly a girly girl.

It had been several years since Blaze had been interested in anyone. She began dating Black, her father's vice president, at a very young age, and their relationship had been toxic, to say the least. Black even proposed to her, and the two of them dreamt of walking down the aisle and then starting a family together. Over time, Black changed and was no longer the caring man she had known him to be in the beginning. The shift started when he became more distant over time, and then the disrespect began. It used to be that everyone else saw his savage side, but when they were together, he was her big teddy bear. Eventually, there was nothing left in him but the savage, and that wasn't something Blaze was going to put up with. She got sick and tired of having to walk on eggshells around him and truly lost herself in their relationship. When Blaze finally got the courage to leave him, she dipped and never looked back. After all the things Black put her through, she learned to build a steel wall around her emotions and her heart. She immersed herself deeply into the club and never dated... period.

"Fuck it," Blaze said aloud to herself. She reached into her closet and grabbed a simple black body-con dress that showed off all her curves. She figured if she was going to metaphorically hop back in the saddle, then she better give it her all.

She walked over to the Bluetooth speaker on the far side of her bedroom and turned it on. A track from Summer Walker started to play, and it consumed her immediately.

Blaze started dancing to the music as she got undressed.

"I know it's been too long. I've been on the road too much. Had to get back to ya, back to youuu," she sang to herself as she stepped in front of her bedroom mirror, admiring every inch of her brown-skinned body.

Blaze made her way to her bathroom when her cell phone rang. She went back to her bedroom and saw that it was Trey calling. She held the phone and let it ring two more times before picking up, trying to ease the butterflies that suddenly appeared in her gut.

"Hello?" Blaze answered in an almost sensual voice.

"Hey, beautiful. I was just checking in on you and making sure we're still good for tonight," Trey replied.

"Yeah. We're still good. I'm actually getting ready now," Blaze replied.

"I have a question, but you have to promise not to bite my head off. I promise my question has a purpose," Trey said. Blaze was immediately skeptical.

"Okay, I'll take the bait… What's your question?" Blaze asked.

"Do you wear weave?" Trey asked.

"What the hell kind of question is that? What? If I do wear weave, you're going to cancel our date or something? This is why I don't give niggas the time of day now. If I wear weave, y'all got something smart to say about it, but if I don't, and I choose to wear my hair natural, then y'all talk shit about that too. I just—"

"Chill, ma. Chill, chill, chill," Trey interrupted while laughing.

"It's nothing like that. I love my sistahs, whether they're natural or rocking that expensive Brazilian shit y'all wear. I promise there's a legitimate reason I asked, but you'll have to wait until later to find out," he continued.

"Yeah... okay ...well, I do wear weave. I don't know why you're asking, but it's not going to fall out randomly or anything. I ride, so I have to keep my weave tight. It's expensive and can last through anything. This lace front ain't going nowhere, trust," Blaze said.

"Alright. That's a bet. Sounds good to me. Meet me at the diner off the main highway," Trey said.

"Okay. I'll meet you there at eight," Blaze said. *He's got some nerve*, Blaze thought. She was glad he couldn't see the expression on her face when he said that they were meeting up to go to a diner. The question about the weave had also blown her. Blaze wasn't about to deal with another one of these shallow niggas that cared more about a woman keeping her hair, nails, and makeup done and always rocking the flyest gear than how loyal or caring she was.

Despite any reservations Blaze may have had, she was still going to go out with this new guy. It had been too long since she had done something like this. The fact that Trey wasn't her type was one of the main reasons she wanted to take the leap. He didn't seem like the usual criminals she dealt with. Who knew what could happen when she decided to step outside the box?

Blaze picked up her towel to head to her bathroom when her cell phone rang again and stopped her in her tracks.

"This is a sign, Blaze. This is a sign," she said aloud to herself.

"Hello!" Blaze answered with a slight attitude.

"Damn, rudeness! I'm always supposed to call and check in

before a run. Remember?" Laila asked on the other end of the phone.

"Oh yeah. My bad, boo. I was just... never mind. It's not important. What's up? Everything good?" Blaze asked. She couldn't believe that in her excitement over her first date in a long time, she almost forgot about the run.

"Yeah. We're about to ride out with the Kings for our first gun drop. Your pops has us playing bike booty this time. We looking like some straight slut buckets, girl. If it wasn't for janky ass Angel volunteering to go, I would damn sure be sitting this one out. Ugh!" Laila said with the upmost disgust dripping from her voice.

"Just do your job, Laila. Damn. It won't be like that every time. Is everybody dressed accordingly?" Blaze asked.

"Yeah. Ass cheeks hanging out, titties up and at attention and all. I even threw a couple red extensions in my ponytail."

"No ponytail, bitch," Blaze said.

"What? Why the fuck not?" Laila protested.

"Think, Laila. It's your signature thing. Either let it all loose and throw some curls in or put on a wig on or something. You and that ponytail are way too noticeable."

"I am *not* curling my hair like I'm some young ass schoolgirl. I'll take door number two with the wig," she said.

"Okay then... and Laila?" Blaze said.

"What's up, boss lady?"

"Make it look good. To blend in, you have to stick out in their way, if that makes sense. Those type of chicks are extra and thirsty for attention. That's why I wanted y'all to go damn near naked. They hang all over their guy, make out with each other, twerk on bikes... you know what to do," Blaze said.

"Yeah, yeah, yeah... act like thots with no home training who are thirsty for dick and attention... we've got it," Laila said while laughing.

"You stupid. I can't with you, but I got to go. I'm meeting grocery store guy tonight. Call me if anything pops off. I'll keep my phone on loud and close by. If I don't hear from you, I'll check in after my date to make sure everything is all good."

"Alright, Blaze. Don't come home pregnant, best friend!" Laila said, and Blaze hung up while laughing. She put her phone on vibrate so she could finish getting ready, uninterrupted, for her big step into new territory.

CHAPTER 4
DEONTRE

"A MAN WITH CHARM IS A VERY DANGEROUS THING."

Trey hung up his phone after making sure Blaze was coming for sure. He turned the keys to start the engine of his silver Hummer and took off in the direction of the diner where he would be meeting up with Blaze. He wasn't actually taking her on a date to a diner, but Trey knew she would never allow him to come to her house to pick her up, so he didn't even bother mentioning it.

It took Trey about thirty minutes to get to their meeting spot. He sat in the parking lot observing his surroundings, keeping an eye out for a fine woman on a motorcycle. Trey noticed a black truck pull into the parking lot about twenty minutes later and park a few spaces down from him. Trey saw Blaze step out of the truck and look around. She was looking even better than she had on the first day he met her. She was wearing a tight black dress that hugged her curvaceous body in all the right places.

Trey's gold iPhone lit up, alerting him that he had a message, and it snapped him back to reality. He stuck the phone in his glove compartment and grabbed his silver iPhone from the back seat. Trey stepped out of his Hummer and walked toward Blaze's truck. She had her back turned toward him and was scrolling through her phone when he walked up.

"Hey, gorgeous," Trey said, placing his hand on her shoulder. She nearly jumped out of her skin at his touch.

"Shit!" Blaze practically yelled as she whipped around, one of her fists drawing back out of instinct.

"My apologies, beautiful. I didn't mean to scare you," Trey said while taking a step back with his hands up.

"You startled me, but you didn't scare me. There's a difference. I don't get scared, but you're good. I just wasn't paying attention. That's on me," Blaze told him with a side-eye and a smirk.

"Well, I apologize for startling you," Trey replied.

"I hear you and everything, but uhh… I thought I told you to get creative with this date. This diner has good food, but it's not at all what I had in mind. I could've come here alone on a regular day," Blaze said while pointing in the direction of the diner entrance.

"A date with me is an extremely rare occurrence. You should have pulled out all the stops, my guy,"

"Oh no, sweetheart. Our date isn't here. The food is definitely good, but I wouldn't dare insult you like that… not a woman of your caliber," Trey told her.

"Why did we meet here then if this isn't where our date is going to be?" Blaze asked.

"Do you trust me?" Trey asked.

"Hell no I don't trust you! Are you crazy? I just met you, nigga," she responded while looking him up and down.

"You trusted me enough to go out with me alone. I guess the better question is, will you hop in the car with me? I'm sort of trying to impress you here. Can you work with me, baby?" Trey asked while flashing that million-dollar smile that caught Blaze's attention at the grocery store.

"I ain't ya baby yet, but I don't know... You might try something," Blaze said flirtatiously with a smirk.

"I'm sure if I did try something, you could handle yourself very well with that heat you're carrying," he said while looking Blaze up and down. She cocked her head to the side and smiled knowingly at him. Her expression showed she was impressed, to say the least.

"Boot holster?" Trey asked while looking down at the thigh high lace up black boots Blaze was wearing.

"Good guess," Blaze said while checking Trey out at the same time. He was looking extremely handsome in his designer jeans, white Polo shirt, and what appeared to be a very expensive watch. It was very simple and not what she was used to, but it was definitely appealing. The look fit him.

"You're right. I can most definitely handle myself if need be. I'll hop in with you."

She turned back toward her truck and opened the door to grab her diamond studded designer clutch. Trey couldn't help but admire her perfectly round ass as she bent over the seat to reach for it.

"Shall we?" Trey asked while holding out his arm for Blaze to grab. The two walked over to Trey's Hummer, and Trey opened the door for Blaze to get in. When she got in, there was a single long-stemmed rose lying on the dashboard waiting for her. She looked over at Trey while smiling and rolling her eyes.

"What can I say? I'm a bit cliché at times," he said while he laughed and shut the door for her.

"I think I might like cliché," she mumbled under her breath

as she smelled the rose and watched Trey walk around the Hummer to get in. As they drove away from the diner, Trey turned on his radio, and Tank's "When We" started blasting from his speakers.

Blaze stared in Trey's direction with one eyebrow raised and then reached over to turn down the radio. Trey licked his lips and let out a light chuckle.

"Are you going to tell me where we're headed?" she asked.

"Part of my wow factor for the night is going to be using the element of surprise. Good things are even better when you don't know they're coming. Don't you think?" Trey replied.

"I'll take that as a no... you're not telling me where we're going."

"Ding! Ding! Ding! You are correct!" Trey told her while laughing.

"I usually don't like surprises. I was definitely going to text my girls the address of where we're going in case you tried to kidnap me or something, but I'm trying different things these days. You better make it worth my while. How's the saying go? You only get one chance to make a first impression," Blaze said.

"You seem like a woman who is hard to please and enjoys the finer things, so I think you'll enjoy yourself just fine tonight. I'm not worried about that."

"Mmm, I guess you're a fast learner," she told him with a sexy grin. After a few more minutes passed, Trey cut the radio completely off.

"I'm going to have to ask you step out on a limb again and trust me," Trey said. Blaze looked over at him and nodded her head in agreement while admiring his handsome profile, his strong jawline in particular.

"I need you to close your eyes for me," he continued. Blaze leaned in close to him. She was so close he could feel the heat coming from her skin. Looking at Trey, she continued to stare in his direction and then closed her eyes. Trey let out a sexy laugh. A few minutes later, Blaze felt the Hummer come to a stop. Trey allowed the anticipation to build long enough.

"We're here, but keep your eyes closed," Trey instructed. She nodded her head, anticipating what was about to come next. He went around to Blaze's side and helped her out of the Hummer.

"I don't know about this walking with my eyes closed. You better not let me fall. I'd hate to have to two-piece you on our first date."

Both of them laughed, but Blaze's voice got caught in her throat when she felt Trey's hand rest itself on her waist.

"Chill, sweetheart. It's level ground. Just put one foot in front of the other and concentrate on keeping those gorgeous eyes closed. Let me handle the rest."

With a simple head nod, the two proceeded to walk forward until he stopped.

"Okay, Blaze. Open your eyes."

CHAPTER 5
BLAZE

"SHE DIDN'T DARE FLIRT WITH DANGER... UNTIL HIM."

Blaze opened her eyes at Trey's command, and her jaw literally dropped. She was looking at a massive, stunningly beautiful boat. The lighting on the boat made it stand out like a jewel against the night sky. Blaze looked up at Trey and smiled from ear to ear.

"You did alright, I guess." She was trying to keep her composure and still admire what was in front of her, but the truth was, nobody had ever done anything remotely close to this for her. Blaze had never been on a date of this magnitude. When she told Trey to get creative, he had definitely taken heed to her instructions and gone above and beyond. He pulled out all the stops.

"Oh, this old thing? It was nothing," Trey said back to her. She looked over at him, and they both shared another laugh. He reached down and took his shoes off. He looked at Blaze, and she hesitated but then began to follow suit.

"May I?"

Blaze looked at Trey hesitantly but smirked as she watched him kneel down in front of her. Trey unlaced her boots, starting from the top of her thigh and working his way down. He felt her body quiver and saw chill bumps appear on her skin as he allowed his hand to purposely graze the innermost part of her thigh.

He slid off her left boot, but when he got to the right one, he paused and looked up at Blaze. She pulled her pistol from her boot holster before he completely removed it.

"Old habit... I'll put it somewhere safe on the boat," she said to Trey. Blaze got on first, and her heart skipped a beat at the luxurious layout. The large boat was carpeted, and there were lily petals scattered everywhere.

"This is... beautiful, Trey," Blaze said to him in awe.

"I was going to go with rose petals, but I figured that would've been a little predictable, and you told me to get creative. I noticed the lily tattooed on your collar bone, so I assumed lilies mean something to you," Trey said nervously while keeping his eye on her to read her reaction. Blaze quickly turned to look at him. *Where did you come from? Who sent you*, she thought.

"Yeah. You're extremely observant to detail. It's perfect."

Turning to look back at the lily petals, she continued walking. He looked at her and took in the elegance of her features, her perfect bone structure, and the excitement on her face while she looked at the lily petals.

"Are you hungry?" Trey asked. She nodded her head, still slightly in shock, and followed Trey as he descended the stairs into the boat. The downstairs section of the boat was a whole other world. There was a table set up with two covered plates and champagne at the center.

"Okay. This is crazy. What the hell do you do for a living because this is a lot for a first date. What's your poison? Dope dealer? Retired jack boy? Nah. You actually look more like a white-collar crime type of dude. That would make the most sense. Just be honest with me, seriously," Blaze asked.

"You told me that your standards were high and to be creative. I didn't want to come at you half-stepping. I think it's perfect for someone like you. I wanted our first date to be intimate and secluded but show you what I think of you. You're top notch, so you deserve all this. I can tell from the short time I've known you that you have this defensive wall up. You seem really skeptical of everything I do. You're probably used niggas always having an ulterior motive or trying to run game. I want to show you I'm not just running game. I want you to be comfortable around me," Trey answered.

"I get that. You're doing an amazing job too because I can honestly say I've never been on a date like this. No lie, I'm flattered you actually took the time to think things through to make this date special, but you just skirted all around my question like I'd forget. You still haven't told me what you do for a living," Blaze said.

"I work for the city... research and development for different projects... on the architectural end. It's really boring stuff, actually, but I make a killing doing it, so I can't complain. I promise you I'm not into anything illegal, but before we continue, I have one question. While I love the name Blaze, I'm about ninety percent sure that's not the name your parents gave you, so what is your real name?" Trey inquired.

"I guess I've trusted you thus far, so I can trust you with my name. My real name is Egypt Johnson, but a lot of people don't know that, so I would appreciate it if that stayed between us," she answered.

"Egypt... that is a beautiful name. It fits you, but how did you get the nickname Blaze, though? It's kind of unique, so there has to be a story or something behind it," he asked.

How did you get the nickname Trey? Somebody just started calling you Trey one day, right? There's no real story there. Maybe I'm just hot," Blaze said while trying to end that conservation quicker than it had begun. *Why is he so interested in my name?* She figured she was just being paranoid again. It came with the territory of having emotional walls as well as leading the type of life that she did.

"That you are, Blaze. I love the name Egypt, but I'll keep calling you Blaze if you want me to. It's no problem," Trey replied.

"Yeah... I prefer Blaze."

CHAPTER 6
LAILA

"LET'S JUST GET THIS OVER WITH!"

Laila hung up the phone from talking to Blaze. Everything was set for the club's first run of pills and guns. The plan Blaze's father, Anthony, had come up with was brilliant. The product had to get to the beach, and it was Black Bike Week there. The Nubian Riders and the Kings didn't support Black Bike Week because the local vendors there didn't seem to respect the Black dollar, but there was money to be made this year, and the event provided the perfect cover for them. They had no choice but to take advantage of the opportunity.

Laila, Angel, and two other ladies from the Nubian Riders were in the dressing room of Blaze's bar getting their things together for the ride. Laila had on denim cut-off shorts that allowed her ass cheeks to hang out the bottom. She had on a neon pink bikini top and a matching thong that showed whenever she bent over. Angel's outfit was the exact same except her bikini was pink and black.

"Come here," Laila said to Angel. Angel walked over apprehensively with her hands held up, trying to figure out what the issue was. Laila reached down and unbuttoned the top button on Angel's shorts so the top of her bikini bottom showed. Both ladies decided they needed to wear wigs due to Laila's signature ponytail and Angel's noticeable highlights being easily identifiable.

"I can't believe I have to do this," Laila said as she took her ponytail loose and began to wrap her hair.

"Get over it. We're in the same boat," Angel said. She had gotten her hair braided down earlier that day and had already put on her bohemian curl dark brown lace front wig.

"I can't even tell you're... whatever you are... with that on. You just look like a bad ass red bone. You should rock this look more often," Laila said to Angel.

"Damn! Was that an actual compliment coming from you? You must got Ebola or the West Nile shit or something," Angel said playfully as she put the back of her hand on Laila's forehead.

"Funny, but no. Apparently you're here to stay, let Blaze tell it. I can't be an asshole to you all the time... just sometimes," Laila told her with a smirk.

Angel turned to check herself out in the giant mirror. Laila put on what she called her old Ciara wig. It was twenty-two inches long, black, and bone straight with bangs. It always reminded her of the artist Ciara back in the day when she was still hitting the matrix.

"Let's go. We need to be leaving soon," Laila said. All four girls walked out to the bar area where four of the Kings waited with Blaze's father, Anthony. Black was one of them. The guys started to cat-call and whistle when the girls walked out.

"Business!" Anthony said in his booming, commanding voice, and the guys stopped.

"Y'all did a great job with the look, but there's one last thing," Anthony said.

"You may not like it, ladies, but remember... you have to do what you've gotta do. You would be surprised who is paying attention to the smallest details, so you have to wear a property of vest," he added on.

"Yeah fucking right!" Laila cut in.

"Just look at it like role playing," Angel said enthusiastically while picking up one of the vests and putting it on. She gave a flirtatious look to the guy she was going to be riding with.

"Riiiiight..." Anthony said while pausing and looking at Angel sideways with a slight chuckle. Laila snickered at Anthony's expression because Angel was clearly enjoying this dress up thing a little too much.

"Y'all have to realize that dodging attention from the police isn't your only issue. You have got to watch your back around the locals too. If they think you're there for any other reason than to party, then there could be problems. We're not from there. We don't know how territorial the other crews are over that way. If they see anybody coming to possibly do business, that's cutting into their money, and it won't end well," he continued. Laila didn't say another word about wearing one of the vests.

"And there's one more thing. Before I even say it, I don't want to hear shit about it," Anthony said, as he cut his eyes in Laila's direction.

"The decision was made by Blaze and me that Black and Laila will be riding together. Both of you are the vice presidents of your respective clubs, so you need to be out front, leading the group... together," Anthony told them. Laila rolled her eyes, but she still bit her tongue. She was extremely opinionated when it came to club business, but she knew her limits and knew to never go against direct instructions from both Anthony and Blaze. She felt funny riding with Black after what she had done to him the other night, but at this point, she didn't have a say so in the matter.

"Don't worry, baby doll. I don't bite," Black said while trying to provoke Laila. She grabbed one of the vests and held it up for a better look.

"I feel sorry for the chicks that actually have to wear these because this shit is ugly," Laila said. Anthony continued to coach them. Laila regretted ever volunteering for this run, but she just didn't trust Angel and vowed to herself that she would keep an eye on the girl.

"We're still waiting on the fire power to arrive. They should be here any minute, and then y'all will be riding out. The four MCM book bags over there are for the girls. The clothes in these bags are your product. The pills have been sewn into the hem of everything, so if for some reason y'all get pulled over or searched, everything is all good. You can't tell that there is anything different about the clothes, even up close. All the pants have pain pills, and all the tops have X pills. As soon as y'all check in to the hotel down there, get rid of that shit. The guns will be in the Escalade that Hitta will be following you in," Anthony told them all.

The girls looked toward the end of the bar where an intimidating looking guy wearing a King vest with locs was sitting. They hadn't noticed him before because he hadn't made a sound the entire time, but at the mention of his name, he threw up one hand. Hitta made eye contact with Laila and gave her a curt little nod, and she returned it. His mysterious aura was alluring to her, but she directed her gaze elsewhere because she knew she had to focus on the task at hand.

After Anthony was finished briefing the group, they went out back to get ready to head out. Hitta disappeared during the meeting but was waiting for the rest of the group outside when they went around back. Anthony looked at him with a raised eyebrow, and Hitta gave him a small salute, letting him know the guns arrived and been stored in the Escalade, out of sight.

Each couple mounted their bikes together. Laila and Black met at his bike and paused. Laila put on a helmet and her book bag. Laila noticed that Black couldn't help but admire her ass in the shorts she was wearing. His eyes made their way up to her breasts that sat up perfectly perky in her pink bikini. She may not have really been his property, but for the next couple of hours, she would be playing the role, and he was going to enjoy it as much as possible. When Black finally looked up at Laila's face, she was already looking at him with pursed lips. Black getting caught checking her out had apparently snapped him back to reality.

"Hurry up," Black told Laila angrily. Laila rolled her eyes for the thousandth time that night and hopped on Black's bike behind him to ride away.

CHAPTER 7
BLAZE

"EXCUSE ME IF I GET TOO DEEP."

"Dinner was amazing. Crab-stuffed lobster? I loved it. I don't say this often, but I have to admit you've really impressed me tonight," Blaze said while sitting back in her chair. She folded her napkin and placed it on top of her plate.

"I would say my mission is accomplished then. I can finally chill out a little now that I have the queen's approval," Trey said jokingly. He may have been joking, but after Blaze's reassurance that he had done an exceptional job thus far, he appeared visibly more relaxed.

"Are you ready for some champagne?" Trey suggested.

"Champagne? That's a little bit unusual for a first date. Are we celebrating something?" Blaze asked curiously.

"We are celebrating the beginning of a very promising thing," Trey answered.

"I see you're real sure of yourself. I'm with that. I'll definitely drink to that," Blaze replied. Trey stood up and grabbed two champagne glasses out of a cabinet behind him. He set one of the glasses on the table and was about to pour when he paused and turned to Blaze.

"How about we go out on the deck and enjoy the breeze and the view of the water," Trey proposed. Standing up without a word, Blaze grabbed the champagne bottle from Trey.

"I'm going to do something I usually don't do. I'm always in control, so I'll follow your lead," Blaze answered. Trey looked at her sideways and smiled, showing those sexy pearly whites. They made their way to the deck of the boat, and Blaze was glad Trey made the suggestion. The weather was perfect, a summer night with a cool breeze coming from the water's surface. The lighting was mesmerizing. They were alone on the water, but the boat had lights in the floor as well and coming from the railing. The two of them walked to the rail to look out over the water. Trey held out the glasses, and Blaze poured.

"Why didn't you come on your motorcycle tonight?" Trey asked Blaze. She paused as a small flutter in her gut caught her attention. Laila's voice popped in her head and made her think. *When you get a bad feeling about going somewhere or that something isn't right about a person, then you have got to pay attention to that feeling because that shit is real.*

"I wanted—"

Suddenly, it was like her sub-conscious had caught on before her conscious mind did. That flutter in her gut was for a reason, and Blaze couldn't help but question him.

"How did you know I have a motorcycle?" Blaze responded with suspicion all over her tone and expression.

"You told me, remember? When I asked you about your weave? I asked you that because of us being on the boat. Now you see why I couldn't explain. I just wanted to make sure the breeze blowing, and the humidity wouldn't be a problem, but I wanted to keep my plan a secret too," he said.

"Okay... I guess that makes a little sense. That question kind of had me twisted, but that was actually considerate of you." Blaze laughed, brushing off the feeling in her gut that had just been there moments ago.

"As far as my motorcycle... it's kind of weird, but..."

"It's okay. You can tell me. I've heard some pretty weird shit in my day, so go ahead," Trey said.

"Okay, so... The way you look at me makes me feel like a thousand percent woman for some reason. I feel gorgeous, sexy, and desirable. I'm all those things. Don't get me wrong, but my motorcycle represents a whole other side of me. That side is commanding, vicious, and doesn't give a damn about the rules... like an outlaw. That side of me lives by her own rules. I just wanted to feel normal with you... a little soft and not so fierce like I usually do, so I decided to separate my bike from the equation so you can get to know the gentle side of me," Blaze told him.

"That's not weird at all. Although I can't imagine you being vicious or anything like that, I'm flattered you wanted to feel sexy around me, but you're sexy regardless."

"Damn, I can't believe I actually told you that," Blaze said while looking away from him and taking another sip.

"It must be the champagne getting to me. I don't tell just anybody stuff like that about me, especially when we barely know each other," she continued.

"We're here to get to know each other. I just want you to feel like you can come to me about anything and know I'll never judge you for it. Hopefully, you'll be able to think of me as more than *just anybody* one day," Trey said to her.

"I have a question for you, Trey."

"Anything," he replied while leaning in slightly.

"Do you have an escape? Like... something that you do that allows you to step out of your element and be a different person for a second?" Blaze asked.

"I do, actually. Work can get so stressful sometimes..." he began as he took a large gulp of champagne.

"... and tiring. Having to watch your back constantly... your life being in danger... that shit gets old real fast. Being in the company of a breathtakingly gorgeous woman such as yourself takes my mind away from all of that. Being around you, I can feel like a normal person if only for just a moment," Trey said.

Blaze placed her hand on his cheek, and he grabbed her hand and kissed it. That feeling in her gut came back, but between the amount of champagne she already had and the heat that was slowly beginning to grow between her thighs because of it, that fluttery feeling telling her that something was off about her date was practically unnoticeable at this point.

"I didn't realize working for the city could be so daaaangerous," Blaze said while giggling. Trey averted his eyes from hers, realizing he almost said too much. Blaze was a little past tipsy at this point and didn't notice his look or body language change.

"We're getting real deep on the first date, huh? I'd hate to see what would happen if we finished the bottle," Blaze told him, baiting him in. Trey looked at her in that moment and downed the rest of the drink in his glass.

"You want to finish the bottle and see then?" Trey asked. Blaze picked up the champagne bottle and filled Trey's glass to the rim. Then she turned the entire bottle up to her lips without breaking his gaze. Trey set his glass down and grabbed the bottle from Blaze, following her lead and drinking straight from it while looking into her eyes.

Trey took a step toward Blaze, and she didn't move. The closer he got to her, the more he could notice the rise and fall of her chest speed up. In what seemed like the blink of an eye, the two of them were chest to breasts. Blaze looked up at Trey with lust in her eyes, and at that moment, he grabbed the back of her neck and leaned down while pulling her in for a kiss. Their tongues twisted and turned with one another for what seemed like forever until Trey broke away, leaving Blaze standing there practically panting. Blaze looked at him completely confused.

"Are you sure? You've had more than a lot to drink. Maybe we should—"

Trey was cut off in the midst of his *I'm trying to be a gentleman* speech when Blaze reached down and gripped his already erect manhood that was begging to be released from the confinement of his jeans.

Trey grabbed Blaze by the hand and led her to the head of the boat where the lighting was the most beautiful. He backed her up until she was leaning up against the railing. Trey took off his shirt first, and Blaze was in awe. The way his abs were perfectly sculpted and fused down into a V-cut right at his waistline made her inner lips throb. Blaze's eyes made their way up to his solid biceps, and she ran her hands over them, imagining what it was about to be like to grab hold of them as he dove deep inside of her. The fact that he had no tattoos covering them multiplied the effect of his smooth brown skin under the boat's lighting and the moon.

Blaze turned around for Trey to unzip her dress. Trey pulled the sleeves of her dress down over her shoulders and allowed it to fall to her ankles. He stepped back for a moment to take in her undeniable beauty. Her body was even more perfect without clothes. Blaze turned back around to face Trey. He stepped toward her, and their lips locked again.

Grabbing one of Trey's hands, Blaze guided it between her legs and let out a soft moan when his finger found its way inside her honey pot. She was damn near dripping from the anticipation. Sliding a second finger within her and using his thumb to rub circles on her clit, Trey never broke their kiss. Unable to concentrate on what her mouth was doing, Blaze's lips simply hovered in front of Trey's, gasping and panting against his mouth as she felt herself already close to climax. Her moans grew louder on the deck of the boat, and as soon as he felt her thighs quiver, he literally swept her off her feet in one swift motion.

"No. Please, don't stop... please," she whispered against his lips.

"Shhhh."

Blaze wrapped her legs tightly around his waist and locked tongues with him again until she felt something cool touch her from behind. Trey lowered her on to the railing of the boat, and she clung tighter to him.

"Wait. This isn't—"

"Shhhh," Trey commanded again, interrupting her objections. Blaze looked into his eyes, and her nervousness of hanging over the water began to dissipate a little.

"Trust me," Trey told her in a soft, low tone. Blaze reached down to unbutton his jeans while he supported her on the railing, and he allowed his pants to hit the deck of the boat. Blaze pulled his boxers down, and her jaw dropped. His member appeared and bounced like it had hydraulics due to its weight. This man was too good to be true. He was fine, had a great job that made good money, really knew how to woo a woman, and now she saw he had a picture-perfect dick too.

Trey reached down and slowly circled her pink pearl again with the tip of his finger. She leaned her head back, allowing the cool breeze and mist from the water to kiss her skin. As Blaze closed her eyes, enjoying the feeling of her building orgasm again, Trey took that opportunity to slide his now throbbing dick inside of her wetness. She gasped for air and let out a low moan as he gently fucked her with the first five inches of his dick to get her used to his size. Blaze felt Trey go as deep as he could, putting all ten inches in her center, and then he paused. He was caught off guard by how tight and wet her pussy was. She squeezed her walls even tighter around his dick as her eagerness grew.

"What you waitin' for? Get this pussy. We already went this far, Trey. Fuck me like you love me," she whispered in his ear. He started stroking her slow and deep, and her moans filled the night sky. The fact that she was suspended in the air over the water heightened her pleasure even more. Trey was spellbound at how amazing Blaze's pussy was.

"Damn. This pussy too good… fuck," he said lowly. He buried his head into her neck to keep himself from crying out along with her. He couldn't let her know her body already had that power over him.

Blaze's breathing got fast and labored as she started to fuck him back.

"Shit!" she cried out. Blaze rotated her hips as she sat balanced on the rail until he lifted her up. Trey cupped her ass in his hands and moved her up and down on his dick with ease, taking complete control. Blaze hung on to him and enjoyed the ride as she watched his powerful arms flex with each stroke.

"I'm— about— to cum!" Blaze whimpered between breaths.

"Let's cum together, baby," Trey replied in a faint tone. She leaned in to kiss him, but at that exact moment, her change in position caused him to hit her G-spot. Blaze abruptly gasped for air, and he cut off the scream that was about to follow with his tongue in her mouth. Her legs trembled, and he sped up his thrusts. Blaze bit down on his lip as her climax was almost too much for her to handle. Trey exploded inside her and let out the low moan that he had been suppressing from the moment he entered her warm wet center. The sounds were music to both of their ears.

"Gahdamn, Blaze!" he damn near shouted in an exhausted voice. All Blaze could do was smile as a high that was equivalent to taking a blunt to the face for the first time took over her entire body. They looked into each other's eyes and laughed. After pecking her on the lips, Trey lifted Blaze from his manhood, and she let out a slight moan due to the lingering sensitivity. Once she was lowered back down, allowing her feet to touch the deck, she couldn't believe she just had sex on the first date.

You are such a hoe, she thought as she shook her head and let out a light nervous laugh at herself. She bent over uncertainly to scoop up her dress, not knowing what to think after giving herself to Trey so effortlessly and completely.

"Leave it," Trey told her while grabbing her hand. She looked at him with confusion in her expression.

"We're not going to need our clothes tonight."

Blaze smirked and shook her head, following him downstairs and preparing herself for a night full of passion.

CHAPTER 8
LAILA

"FORBIDDEN FRUIT IS SAID TO BE SWEETER, BUT IT ALSO SPOILS FASTER."

The four coupled riders made it safely to the beach and went straight to the hotel as instructed. After checking in, they made their way upstairs to the two rooms they rented. As soon as Laila got inside hotel room, she snatched off her *property of* vest, throwing it on one of the chairs, and Angel followed suit.

"We'll stay here and start cutting up the clothes to get the pills out," Laila said, motioning to the other women.

"And y'all can go ahead and make that gun drop with Hitta. Call us when you're done, and we'll meet up to go down to the beach and get rid of these pills and shit. The quicker we do this, the better," Laila said while giving Black the side eye.

"Aight. Cut the attitude, Laila. If anybody should be pissed off that we have to work together, it should be me. I don't wanna be around yo' ass either, but we gotta work together to make this money smoothly," Black said. Laila was half paying him any attention when she walked to the bathroom to check her makeup.

"Nobody should know we're here, but if y'all have any problems, just call, and we'll come right back," Black said. He got momentarily distracted as Laila turned around, and he had a chance to admire her ass in those tiny booty shorts again. Laila noticed Black checking her out from his reflection in the mirror and laughed to herself.

"Go ahead. We'll call you if anything happens, Daddy," Laila said in a high-pitched voice, trying to entice Black and make fun of him at the same time. Angel looked over at Laila, shaking her head.

"You funny. Chill with all that Daddy stuff," Black responded. Everybody in the room was looking back and forth between the two. Laila sensed the eyes that were on them and decided to make light of the situation.

"Get gone, nigga. I was just playing 'cause we gotta pretend to be y'all little girlfriends. Damn. I don't want yo' medium ugly ass for real," Laila replied.

"Medium ugly?" Angel snorted while trying to suppress a laugh. Black and the other Kings left to go meet up with their mysterious brother, Hitta, to get rid of the guns they had. The other two girls that had come went to the room next door, leaving Laila and Angel alone.

"You ready to pop that cherry, Angel?" Laila asked as she grabbed one of the book bags.

"Just tell me what I need to do," Angel said while sitting down on one of the beds. Laila opened the bag and pulled out seemingly normal clothes, spreading them on the bed. There were mostly tank tops and baby tees. Laila unzipped an outside pocket on the book bag and pulled out two pairs of seam rippers.

"Okay, so everything in here has been double-hemmed. The pills are hidden inside the hem. All you got to do is take this sharp point right here, stick it right below that top stitch line, and slide it across. Make sure you stay under that top stitch, and the pills will fall right out," Laila instructed. She watched as Angel grabbed one of the pairs of seam rippers and did the same with her bag, emptying the contents onto the bed.

"Okay... fucking arts and crafts... great," Angel said sarcastically.

"You joking now, but this is putting money in our pockets and all our sisters, too. Instead of being a smart ass, you better get to cutting because we have to finish before the Kings get back. Don't forget, newbie, I'm still the vice president. Even if I wasn't, I will beat that ass if you fuck up the club's money in any way. Know that! You shouldn't have volunteered if you were gonna talk shit the whole time. Just do the job and shut the fuck up," Laila added.

"I'm not afraid of you, Laila. If you think you're going to run over me, you thought wrong," Angel spat back.

"You can be the bravest mothafucka in the world and still get yo' ass whooped, little girl. They call me Laila for a reason. You know the story, so don't try me," Laila replied nonchalantly while sitting back on the bed.

"Have you been tested for mental illness? I swear yo' ass is bipolar. We were just laughing and kicking it, and you even complimented me."

Laila simply scoffed and continued with the task at hand. Angel shook her head and did the same.

For the next hour, Laila and Angel sat, getting the product together. Aside from the TV playing, the room was silent because neither Laila nor Angel said another word to each other the entire time. Laila's phone rang, and she got up to step outside and answer it. She looked down to see the name *Stupid*

Ass flashing on her screen. She laughed aloud to herself seeing the name pop up because she knew it was Black calling.

"What up?" Laila answered.

"Y'all done?" he asked.

"Yeah. Angel is cleaning everything up now. Everything separated and bagged. We good," Laila told him.

"I need you to come downstairs really quick," Black said.

"Just me? For the fuck what? Hell no, nigga. I don't trust your ass. What do you want?" Laila hissed.

"Look. We had to keep a few of the guns because the guys we're meeting up with to unload the product are affiliated... bloods maybe... and we're not going down there naked and shit. I need you to come get the heat because it's a lot of activity going on in the parking lot, and five niggas with no females in sight is looking real suspect right now," Black explained to her.

"Okay. I'll be there in a minute." Laila sucked her teeth and rolled her eyes dramatically as she hung up. She went back in the room to find that Angel had cleaned up everything and was putting the baggies of the separated pills back into one of the book bags.

"I'll be right back," Laila told Angel. She grabbed the *property of* vest and put it back on.

"Everything good?" Angel asked, looking at Laila sideways.

"Yeah. We good. Just be ready to leave soon," Laila told her while walking out the door. She looked down over the balcony and saw the Kings' bikes and Hitta's Escalade. Laila made her way down the stairs and was immediately annoyed when she didn't see anyone. This was a business trip. There was no time for games. Laila pulled out her cell phone and was about to call Black to curse him out when she felt a large hand grab her by the shoulder. Laila swung around with her strong right hook and made contact with Black's chest.

"Damn, slugger!" Black said while laughing and coughing a little from the impact of her blow.

"Black, you play too fucking much! Shit!" Laila said, panting. As soon as she felt someone grab her, adrenaline rushed through her body. She always swung first and asked questions later.

"I just saw you walking toward the bikes. I didn't mean to scare you, honestly," Black told her while holding up his hands. Laila looked him up and down, still skeptical.

"I stepped back over there for two seconds to buy a drink, and when I saw you, I came straight over. No bullshit," Black told her, pointing to some vending machines that were nearby.

"Where is everybody?" Laila asked with some uncertainty. Black threw up his hands, motioning to some groupies the guys were chatting it up with at the far end of the parking lot.

"Hitta is sitting in the Escalade. We don't need you to take it upstairs anymore because the meet got pushed up," Black said. Laila noticed him looking past her for a minute until he spoke.

"Hey... I know you don't trust me, but whatever you do, don't freak out at what's about to happen. Just play along with it," Black said all of a sudden while still looking past her. There was a group of guys, possibly locals, grilling the Kings, trying to figure out what their purpose for being there was.

Black grabbed Laila by her ass, gripping it tightly, and pulled her in for a kiss. She quickly caught on and kissed him back. His hands roamed Laila's body, and she laid it on thick, giggling as he aggressively slapped her on the ass and continued to tongue her down. After a few more seconds, Laila opened her eyes and glanced in the direction where the men had been, but they were long gone. Laila tried to break away from Black's embrace, but he held her tighter. The grip of his strong hands on her ass and the forcefulness with which he held her was actually turning her on. Laila got so distracted that she did the unthinkable and began to kiss Black again, only this time it wasn't acting. Black wrapped his muscular arms around her and held her close as their tongues danced.

Laila was feeling so good in Black's arms and got lost in her own rising arousal until someone in the parking lot revved their bike, and she snapped back to reality. She looked up into his eyes and remembered where she was and what she was doing. She bit Black's lip hard enough to get him off her.

"Keep this shit up, and you'll be coming back from this trip with one less ball, nigga. I'm serious. Quit fucking playing with me," Laila fussed as she punched him on the shoulder.

"Don't act like you haven't seen me checking you out. You know that shit felt good, girl. We grown. You can be for real," Black said while looking her up and down with lust in his eyes.

"You can get that shit out of your mind right now because nothing is going down between us, Black," Laila told him.

"Yeah. That's what ya mouths says, but the way yo' tongue was all in mouth just now says different."

Black stepped closer to Laila yet again, and she surprisingly didn't move.

"And that pussy don't agree with you either. I can tell by the way you were squirming in my arms that she soaking wet right fuckin' now," Black added, and the tone of his voice sent a shiver down her spine. Taking a step back to collect herself, she slowly turned away from Black.

She was genuinely shocked at what she had just done. Laila had to remind herself to stay focused on the task at hand. She made her way to the side of the building to go back upstairs and get the rest of the girls when she saw Angel peeking out at the two of them from the hotel window with a phone to her ear. Angel quickly let the curtain close as Laila looked back over at Black. She could only hope Angel wouldn't let the cat out the bag about what she just witnessed.

CHAPTER 9
DEONTRE

"EVEN THE PEOPLE WHO BETRAY YOU ARE A PART OF THE MASTER PLAN."

Trey and Blaze were lying on a couch downstairs on the boat, having just made love for a third time.

"I can't believe we did that," Blaze said while caressing Trey's abs.

"It's sounds so cliché that I almost don't want to say it, but I've never done this before. Seriously, I'm not that girl," Blaze told him, and they both burst out laughing.

"What's done is done, and I don't think any less of you, if that's what you're worried about," Trey told her while caressing her shoulder.

"We're grown, and I don't regret anything," he added. Blaze was just about to sit up and steal another kiss from Trey when his phone rang. He looked at the name on the screen of his phone and nudged Blaze out of the way so he could get up from the couch.

"My bad, baby. I've got to take this. It's work... clients in other time zones... they don't think about that sometimes," Trey said while heading toward the stairs.

He felt Blaze's eyes follow him all the way up the stairs until he was out of sight. When Trey felt like he had gotten out of Blaze's earshot, he glanced over his shoulder and then answered.

"What are you doing calling me right now? This had better be good, Angel," Trey said.

"Check the attitude. Don't forget who's doing who a favor," Angel shot back.

"I've got something interesting. You know the guy Black you were looking into? It turns out that's Blaze's ex-boyfriend... Oh, shit!" Angel said all of a sudden.

"What happened?" Trey whispered into the phone.

"I don't have long now. I think Laila just caught me watching her. What I was going to tell you was I think there's something going on with Blaze's best friend and Black, and in this club, everything revolves around sisterhood and loyalty and all that shit. I just saw them kissing, and it looked like it was about to get pretty steamy. It may be nothing, but to me, it seems like there's trouble in paradise between best friends," Angel said while moving closer to the bathroom and keeping an eye on the door.

"No. That's definitely something. This is your chance to get closer to Blaze because if she were to somehow accidently find out that her best friend is fooling around with the man that used to be the love of her life, there will be a vacancy in her life... an open position for a new right hand," Trey said in a hushed voice while looking in the direction of the boat's stairs.

"Okay. I've got to go. I'll keep you posted," Angel said and hung up. Trey hung up the phone and immediately put it on airplane mode. He could tell Blaze had been suspicious of the call, especially being that he let her know upfront he was single and wasn't in the streets. He couldn't risk taking a private call around her again if he wanted her to open up to him quickly.

Trey headed back downstairs to join Blaze on the couch. When he got to the bottom of the steps, he saw her sitting up on the couch, partially dressed.

"I apologize for that. Work won't interrupt us again," he said while sitting down next to her.

"It's okay, Trey. I actually should get going," Blaze told him.

"It's late. You might as well stay the rest of the night," Trey said while trying to pull her closer.

"I have something I need to take care of. It's just work stuff," she said while smirking and standing up. She leaned back down to peck him on the lips.

"What kind of work do you do, if you don't mind me asking?" Trey asked curiously.

"I own a bar. You may not have heard of it because it's a pretty low-key spot for the most part... Leather and Lace?" Blaze asked.

"Low-key? No. I've definitely heard of it and the infamous Summer Kick-Off every year. I've heard a lot of stories about that place. I had no idea who the owner was. I almost came this year. What are the odds of that?" Trey asked.

"Yeah... what are the odds?" Blaze replied.

CHAPTER 10
ANGEL

"BE CAREFUL HOW YOU TREAD, 'CAUSE EVERY STEP WILL SHOW."

Angel hung up the phone from her conversation with Trey and made sure everything was packed up and ready to go for the drop. As she was double-checking the book bags, she tried to figure out the best way to go about this Laila and Black situation. She had to play her hand smart without showing it if she wanted to win.

Angel figured blackmail would be the best way to go. She couldn't just come out and tell Blaze about her best friend and ex were possibly having a fling behind her back. Blaze and Laila had a lifetime of trust and loyalty built up. Even if they didn't have that bond, if Angel went straight to the boss lady and told her what happened, none of the other club members would ever trust her. Angel would be seen as a snitch, no matter the circumstances under which it was done. She would have to let Laila know that she was aware of her and Black's indiscretion and allow the hatred that Laila already had for her to do the rest of the work. The more Laila would try to push Angel out, the further she would eventually push herself away from Blaze.

Angel's thoughts were interrupted by Laila storming through

the door and coming across the room, going straight for her neck.

"Look here, mothafucka!" Laila started off while trying to choke the life out of Angel.

"I don't know what you were doing spying on me, who you were talking to on that phone, or what you think you saw, but if you say one word to Blaze or anybody else, I will fuck that pretty face of yours up beyond recognition. Do you understand me, bitch?" Laila asked through gritted teeth, almost in a whisper. Angel nodded her head in agreement and gave Laila a look through watery eyes that said she was begging to be released. Laila released Angel just as Black was walking back into the room.

"Y'all ready? Everybody else is waiting downstairs," he said while looking back and forth between the two.

"Yeah... we're coming," Laila said as she picked up the other *property of* vest and threw it forcefully at Angel. Black looked at Angel, who was glaring at Laila while rubbing her throat. He looked back and Laila while laughing to himself and shaking his head.

"Aye, get everything. We're not coming back," Black shot over his shoulder on his way back out the door. With one last menacing look at one another, Laila and Angel grabbed the bags and headed out the door to get to the money.

CHAPTER 11
BLAZE

"KARMA HAS NO DEADLINE."

When Trey finally got Blaze back to her car and they said their goodbyes, she took a moment to gather her thoughts. Her one-of-a-kind date had momentarily made her forget about the club, the guns, and the drugs, but she snapped back to reality when she checked her phone and saw ten missed calls and several text messages from Laila, Black, and her father.

"Shit!" Blaze said aloud to herself. She clicked on the voicemail icon and saw that a message was waiting from Laila:

Laila: Boss lady! We're heading back. We'll be back at the bar in a few hours. Everything went... well. Meet me there to deposit our cut. Hope you didn't do anything I wouldn't do.

Blaze locked her phone, started up her truck, and headed back to the club. Laila left the message a few hours ago, so she would probably get there at the same time as them.

The whole ride over, Blaze couldn't help but to think about her night with Trey. All her life, she had been attracted to bad boys like Black, but this one seemed different. He actually put forth effort for the first date, instead of the men who usually asked her out and just wanted to chill at her place or theirs. Despite how well the date had gone and how much she was feeling Trey, she did sincerely regret sleeping with him. Blaze frankly wasn't that type of female to drop her panties on the first date.

Her mind wandered to those fluttery feelings she experienced when she was with Trey, and they weren't the hopeful butterfly flutters. It was all about vibrations, and the vibe she was getting from Trey was off for some reason, but until he showed her otherwise, she was going to continue to see him.

Blaze didn't have much time to think about her eventful night once she pulled up to the club. Along with everyone else's bikes that had gone on the drop, she saw her father's motorcycle among them. This was unusual for her father, unless something bad happened during the run. She quickly parked and got out of her truck, hoping that no one was hurt or locked up. She switched out of her thigh high boots for her riding Polo boots before going inside. Blaze walked in to see Laila and Black counting money in the corner, and the other Kings were shooting pool and having a few beers.

"How did everything go?" she asked. Black turned, and his eyes got big at the sight of Blaze in her tight dress that left nothing to the imagination and her boots. Black was definitely an ass and leg man. He was looking her up and down, and she could tell he was wondering where she was coming from dressed like that. She subconsciously ran her hand over her hair, smoothing it down as if it was still all over the place after her multiple sex sessions with Trey.

"Everything went smoothly," Laila said while cutting her eyes toward Angel who was seated at the bar.

"But look at you! Boss lady is looking sexy tonight," Laila added while checking her best friend out.

"Cut it out, girl," Blaze said while glancing over at Black to see if he was still paying attention to her.

"Good job, everybody. Soon as our VPs are done counting up, you can get your cut of the money and head home... or you can chill for a while. I'll keep the spot open for whoever wants to hang out and wind down or if you need to crash and head home in a few hours," Blaze added as she looked around and noticed two of the Kings joined Angel at the bar and had clearly just begun drinking.

"Aye, Laila, where's my pops? Did he say why he came here? Is everything good?" Blaze asked.

"Oh, yeah. He's in the back office. He said he needed to talk to you and that it was urgent. He said he tried you on your cell, but he couldn't get you," Laila said while smirking at Blaze. They licked their tongues out at one another, and Blaze walked off, heading toward the office in the back.

Blaze walked inside the office to see her father sitting at the table with a concerned expression on his face.

"Shut the door," he instructed her in a worried voice. Blaze did so and walked over to her father quite confused and nervous. She took a seat at the table beside Anthony.

"What's wrong, Pops? Did something happen?" she asked.

"I got a disturbing call from the lawyer today," he said with a serious look on his face.

"She told me there's been a buzz going around between her contacts in the FBI... A local cold case file was recently reopened," Anthony told her. As soon as Blaze heard that, her heart nearly stopped.

"What... file? What does this mean for us?" she stuttered out.

"It was a murder investigation from sixteen years ago. I don't know why this is suddenly coming up now, but I have to ask. Have you been making any new friends lately, received any mystery calls, or had someone pop up at the club asking questions?" Anthony asked. Blaze's mind immediately went to Trey, but she brushed it off.

"Nah, Pops. Nothing like that. I haven't said anything to anyone... ever, not even Laila. I know the deal. If me, you, or Black ever talk about it, we would all go down," she answered.

"Okay, I'll keep you updated. For now, just be careful of everything... what you say on the phone, where you go, and who you hang around," Anthony told her as he stood up.

"Yes, sir," Blaze replied as Anthony stood up over her and kissed her on her forehead.

"I already spoke with Black. He knows what's up, so I'll leave everyone to unwind after their successful run. I'm about to take my money and dip!" Anthony said while standing up and putting his shades on.

"It's nighttime. What's with the shades, old man?" Blaze asked her dad.

"If you must know, I have a date," he said. Blaze twisted up her face and burst out laughing.

"And I don't want all this handsome to overwhelm her at once. I'm not just president of the Kings, I'm president of the beautiful people club, too. You better act like you know! Where do you think you got all your swag and good looks from?" Anthony asked while stroking his salt and pepper goatee and giving a deep, hearty laugh.

"Am I on fleek tonight, baby girl?" he asked while posing and flexing his muscles.

At this point, Blaze was in tears from laughing at her father.

"Pops, don't ever... ever, ever, ever... say fleek again," she told him in between her laughter.

"Just go on to your lil' booty call. Tell our lawyer... I mean your girlfriend I said hey," Blaze added with a smirk.

"Mind your business, young'n!" Anthony said on his way out the door.

Blaze stayed in the office for a few minutes after Anthony left, just reflecting on what he told her. No one knew about the past except her, Black, and her father, and they had all vowed to take that secret to the grave, but something was going on. Even though she tried to push the thought from her mind, Trey kept coming to the forefront as if her subconscious was trying to tell her something, but she wouldn't let Anthony know about him just yet. She didn't want him to worry for no reason, and on top of that, she really liked Trey. She didn't want to believe he had any ties to the same type of life she lived.

The saying went *keep your friends close and your enemies closer.* Blaze wasn't sure if Trey would turn out to be an enemy, but he was definitely new and would be treated accordingly. She figured she would do a little digging into him as soon as she got the chance, just to ease her own suspicions.

A knock interrupted Blaze's thoughts. It was Angel at the door.

"Hey, Blaze. We're all pretty wired up and wanted to hang out for about another hour. Want to take a shot with me?" Angel asked.

"Sure, girl. I'm coming," Blaze told her, and they went to the bar to toast to getting money and new friendships.

CHAPTER 12
DEONTRE

"LIFE IS THE ART OF BEING WELL DECEIVED."

Trey woke up around lunchtime the day after his date with Blaze. His job was to get close to Blaze and get her to trust him and begin to open up to him. Right after he fucked Blaze, he knew he had taken it too far. At one point, after the champagne started to get to him, he almost let his true occupation slip out. He had no idea when he signed up for this that he would be so physically attracted her and drawn to her personality. Trey knew he had to put his own feelings to the side and play his role. He had to focus on the end game and not how sexy she looked or how good her pussy was for that matter.

Trey's phone rang. He picked it up, and it was Blaze.

"Hello?" he answered.

"Hey... you sound half sleep. I didn't wake you, did I?" she asked.

"Oh, no. I've been up for a while. What's good?" he asked, sitting all the way up and rubbing his eyes.

"I just wanted to touch bases with you. I hate that I had to dip out on you all of a sudden last night. I didn't want you to think it was anything you did because you were... amazing doesn't even describe. I didn't want it to cause any awkwardness between us," she told him.

"It's all good, baby. Trust me. If there's anyone who can understand how it is when work comes up, it's me. I was actually going to call to see if you wanted to hang out today... just dinner, nothing more," Trey offered while laughing nervously.

"Yeah. You're right about the nothing more part. I would love to go to dinner, but we need to take like ten steps back. I know I'm sounding so cliché again, but no man has ever made me feel—Mmmm."

Trey pulled the phone away from his face and looked at it with a knowing grin, realizing Blaze just had a momentary flashback of their night together when she accidently let out a soft moan.

"Well, damn. We should—"

"Shouldn't have done it!" she interrupted, not wanting the conversation to go down the route of discussing what happened for fear that she'd lose control again when she saw him.

"Sex complicates things when you're actually trying to get to know someone," Blaze added.

"You're absolutely right. I completely agree. We should take a few steps back. It's whatever makes you comfortable. As long as I still get to see you, I'm good," he replied.

"Great! We can have dinner at your place. I'll bring the wine and a few movies, and you can cook."

Trey hesitated at the mention of Blaze coming to his place to chill.

"Me? Cook? I don't want to sound sexist but shouldn't the woman in the equation be doing the cooking?" he asked.

"Well, yes. You sounded absolutely sexist," Blaze told him while laughing.

"A man that can cook is a requirement for me. You want to see me? Sometimes you're going to have to cook," she admitted.

Trey thought on it for a few seconds, but he figured he had to agree. Blaze might pose more questions if he said she couldn't come to his place.

"It's a date. I guess I better find some good recipes then," Trey added.

"Yeah. You better. Burgers and fries or box macaroni does not count as real cooking in my book. You know how I like it... get creative. Text me your address, and I'll be over around six. Is that time okay with you?" she asked him.

"That time works for me, and hey... since we got the first date out of the way, let's do this a little less formally. You can come in your regular clothes. Dinner will be ready at six, ma'am," Trey said. Blaze laughed at him calling her ma'am.

"There is nothing regular about me, but I get what you're saying. I'll see you at six, sir," she responded and hung up.

Trey looked at his phone and saw that it was already two in the afternoon, so he didn't have much time. He still had to go by the office and then head to the grocery store so he could get the items to cook a satisfactory meal for Blaze. He had just gotten up to get in the shower when his phone rang again. He looked down and saw it wasn't the phone in his hand, but it was his gold iPhone on his dresser.

"What's up, Angel?" Trey answered.

"I have some info, Trey," Angel replied. Trey quickly sat back on the bed.

"Yeah? Tell me what's going on," he said, urging her to go on.

"When we got back from the beach early this morning,

Blaze's father was there waiting for her. They went to the back office, so I followed them and listened at the door. I heard Anthony say something about a cold case. They most definitely know something is going on. I think we should back off for a little while," Angel confessed with a lot of worry in her tone.

"Damn... okay. Just stay close to them," Trey said. He was silent for a few seconds while trying to think what he should do. He still had some questions he needed answered, but he would have to move fast. The smallest mistake right now could cause everything to unravel and fall apart, and Blaze seemed like a smart girl. She would figure out what was going on by herself if he took too long.

"Okay, but just hurry. I'm ready to be done with this shit already," Angel said.

"I've got you. Just stay close to your phone," Trey told her before hanging up. He had to figure out something and fast. Trey ran to take a quick shower and throw on some Nike sweats and a T-shirt. Something had to happen tonight at his and Blaze's informal dinner or else he would end up getting Angel hurt, or worse. He needed to get Blaze to tell her story. Trey grabbed his keys, both of his phones, got his Glock out of his safe, and rushed out the door.

CHAPTER 13
BLAZE

"A HIDDEN TRUTH IS A LIE. OMISSION IS A LIE. A LIE IS A LIE."

Blaze spent most of her day meditating and thinking about the strange happenings of the past few days. It was like one day, she met Trey, and the next day, they had gone from zero to one hundred. She couldn't get him off her mind. Blaze couldn't figure if she was getting caught up in Trey because it had been so long since she had even spent time with a man, especially intimately, or if she was genuinely falling for him this fast. At this point, anybody seemed better than Black. She just didn't want to get caught up in trying to make a lasting relationship with the rebound guy. The fact that she had given up the goods on the first night also served no purpose other than to confuse her more.

Blaze's thoughts were interrupted when she happened to glance at the clock and saw that it was getting close to six.

Blaze thought about what Trey suggested about this date being less formal and figured this time she was going to go with an outfit that was more like her everyday look. She already told Trey they needed to take a few steps back and slow down because being intimate on the first date had been a mistake. She made a mental note not to put on anything too revealing or exceedingly sexy.

Blaze went over to her stereo and turned it on. Kevin Gates and Trey Songz's "Jam" started to play, and she immediately hit the next button. R&B was definitely not what she wanted to listen to before going to see Trey. She wanted to put sex with him in the very back of her mind so she could step back and objectively get to know him better. Maybe it was already a little too late, but if she continued to go there with him, she knew the dick would veil her judgement. Black Youngsta came blaring through her speakers, and she decided to stick with that...

French Montana, no coke boy
Boys in the hood call me dough boy

Blaze sifted through her closet and decided to wear her Leather and Lace club attire. She was going to ask Trey if he wanted to hang out at Leather and Lace after their dinner and let her girls size him up to get their opinions about him.

Blaze put on a black corset-like top, dark denim shorts, and her Polo biker boots. After putting on her Nubian Riders' vest, grabbing her phone and her crossbody Gucci bag, she headed out the door on her way to Trey's place.

The first thing she noticed when she reached her destination was the average-looking neighborhood he lived in. Blaze had been expecting a lot more after the boat date. If he was balling the way he seemed he was, then she would have expected him to be in some type of house or at least a higher-class area. The vibes were off again, and that fluttery feeling was threatening her peace of mind about this guy, but she shook it off since she was already there.

Blaze pulled up beside Trey's Hummer and parked her motorcycle. She pulled out her phone to call and let Trey know that she was coming up, but some sort of feeling deep down told her not to.

Blaze made her way inside his building and headed toward the elevator. On her way up, she made sure her two pistols were secured; the .380 in her boot holster, and the .9mm inside her vest. She may have liked Trey, but she wasn't naïve or just plain stupid. She was the leader of a motorcycle gang that ran drugs and weapons, and she was not going to get caught slipping anywhere, especially not over some new dick.

After entering his building, she headed straight to the elevator. It dinged at the bottom floor, and the doors slid open. She got off on Trey's floor and walked down the hall until she got to the right door. She pulled out her phone and opened her text messages from Trey, double checking that she had the correct apartment. From outside, she could already smell the busy aromas of some appetizing food cooking, so she knew she was in the right place for sure. Blaze knocked on the door, and she heard shuffling inside the apartment.

"Coming!" she heard Trey yell from behind the door. A few seconds later, the door swung open, and Trey was standing in front of her with Jordan shorts on and no shirt. Blaze's eyes quickly traveled over his body. When they landed on his muscular arms, her kitty jumped because just that quickly she had a flashback of when he had been using those arms to lift her up and down on his dick during their first date.

"You have to excuse my appearance. I was getting down in

the kitchen, and I wasn't expecting you for like thirty more minutes," he said, slightly out of breath. Shaking her head to bring herself back to the present, Blaze's eyes met his.

"Mmm hmmm," she commented while looking him up and down with a smirk.

"You might want to go ahead and put on a shirt... just so I'm not tempted," she told him.

"I'll get right on that, but check you out with all your gear on, biker chick," Trey said while checking her out.

"Funny! Now go... shirt," she said, playfully pushing past him and walking inside.

"I'll get right on that," he said while laughing. When Trey went down the hall of his apartment toward what Blaze assumed was his bedroom, she looked around. The inside of the apartment was definitely much nicer than the outside, and all the walls were bare. No artwork, pictures of him or remnants of a family could be found anywhere, which further showcased how off things were. He claimed to have this nice job that made decent money, but he lived in a lower-class neighborhood with upper-class furnishings. Blaze walked toward the living room and noticed there were manila folders spread over his coffee table. Just as she was about to let her curiosity take over, Trey came back with a wife-beater tank top in his hand.

"I'm just going to finish up in the kitchen before I put this on. No flexing... I swear," he told her.

"Yeah, yeah. You just want an excuse to have your shirt off for a little while longer. I'll let you be great. Go ahead," Blaze told him while taking in the image of him shirtless and slightly messy, preparing a meal for her.

"Make yourself at home. You can put on some music if you want," he said while walking back toward the kitchen.

"Music where? There's no stereo system in here. You better not be trying to find an excuse to get me to your bedroom because it's not happening," Blaze told him jokingly. Trey peeked his head out of the kitchen.

"Stereo system? Your age is showing, ma," Trey said before he started laughing.

"Everything is hooked up through my TV and my smart home stuff. There's all different stations; R&B, hip hop, everything... but the way you're dressed tonight looks like you in the mood for some trap music," he said jokingly before stepping back to the oven.

"Very funny!" Blaze yelled from the living room. *He's right, though.* She started flipping through the music stations on Trey's sixty-inch TV, and her eyes shot back over to the folders she noticed a few minutes ago. She took a step toward them while glancing in the direction of the kitchen.

"You almost done in there? A chick is starving in here, and that good smell is making it worse!" Blaze yelled without taking her eyes off the folders.

"Give me like twenty more minutes. I promise it will be worth it. I hear you jamming to the Tupac station, too. I'll join you in a few!" he yelled back. Blaze took that as her green light. Her vibes about the place had been off from the moment she had stepped foot in Trey's apartment. She turned the music up slightly, took one more glance toward the kitchen, and sat down on his new leather couch in front of the coffee table.

"You should come to the club with me for a little while after dinner!" she yelled to the kitchen as she picked up the folders.

"Hell yeah. I get to meet your crew. I'm with that!" Trey yelled back, but Blaze didn't hear a word he had said. Her focus was elsewhere.

Nothing could have prepared Blaze for what she was about to see. She flipped the four folders over and read each tab; Egypt Johnson... Anthony Johnson... Kareem White... Cold case 11415. Blaze felt her heart momentarily stop, and everything suddenly seemed to make sense.

CHAPTER 14
DEONTRE

"FUCK IT. MASK OFF!"

"Give me like twenty more minutes. I promise it'll be worth it. I hear you jamming to the Tupac station too. I'll join you in a few!" Trey yelled. His masterpiece was almost complete. He prepared extra-large manicotti stuffed with lobster and a cheese and garlic sauce on top. The corn on the cob and green beans were already done. Trey glanced at his work phone and turned it off. He knew he was supposed to be getting close to Blaze for information, but that wasn't his purpose tonight. The line had already been crossed on the night of their first date. Being honest with himself, he'd lost sight of his mission the minute their lips met. Trey knew he shouldn't have allowed Blaze into his home or his figurative space, but he couldn't help himself.

"You should come to the club with me for a little while after dinner!" Blaze yelled to the kitchen.

"Hell yeah. I get to meet your crew. I'm with that!" Trey yelled back at her. She was already comfortable with him going to meet her friends. He knew then that she was digging him just as much as he was digging her. There were a few minutes of silence, and he was thinking of peeking around the corner to check on Blaze.

"Smells amazing in here." Trey turned around to see Blaze standing behind him, looking super sexy.

"This is all for you too. I never just cook like this for no reason. Next time will be your turn to spoil me. I can't do all the cooking between the two of us," Trey said.

"Yeah, sure... next time is on me," Blaze said while moving closer to him.

"Aye, don't get too close. You said we needed to slow down so we could get to know each other, but if you get any closer looking as sexy as you do, I don't know if I'll be able to keep that promise," Trey told her while eyeing her up and down and biting his own juicy lip slightly.

"Did I say that? Me? That doesn't really sound like anything I would suggest. I don't remember saying anything like that," Blaze cooed seductively. She gently grabbed him by the hand and guided him to his living room. She walked him over to the couch, allowing him to sit down, and then she straddled him. "Hail Mary" was blasting from Trey's Tupac station.

Blaze leaned down and kissed on Trey's neck while rubbing her hands over his perfectly sculpted chest. *This is some gangsta ass shit. Damn... is she gon' fuck me to some Tupac? I think I might be in love for real,* Trey thought, chuckling internally and enjoying the sensation of her hands roaming over his body.

Trey gripped her ass as his dick swelled beneath her. His eyes fell upon his coffee table, which was completely clean. He had to think to himself if he left some papers laying out or not. Panic started to set in because he couldn't remember if he scooped the papers up before he opened the door and let her in a few minutes ago. The concern immediately left his mind because there was no blood left in his brain. Blaze reached down into Trey's Jordan shorts and started stroking his dick with her hand, and he forgot about his slip up just that quick.

Trey leaned his head back and closed his eyes as he prepared himself to be rode all the way to ecstasy. With his eyes still closed, he felt Blaze's lips meet his once again, and his mind seemed to go blank. His purpose for even running into her that day at the grocery store, along with everything he stood to lose if things went left, completely left his mind. This woman had just that much power over him with a simple kiss.

Suddenly, Trey's heart sank to his stomach as he felt cold steel against his temple. He opened his eyes to see Blaze holding his dick in one hand and a nine-millimeter in the other, pointed at his skull.

"Who... the fuck... are you?" she asked through gritted teeth while cocking the hammer back and pressing the gun harder into his head. Trey was frozen. He knew he fucked up. Everything became crystal clear with that beautiful piece of heat pointed at his dome. He left his case files laying out in the open for her to see like a dumb ass. He let his guard down and gotten caught slipping because he was actually catching feelings for a suspect. He had possibly fucked up months of the bureau's work because of his carelessness.

"You're a gahdamn FBI agent! Aren't you? Aren't you!" she yelled, pushing the barrel of the gun harder into his skin, leaving an indentation.

"Egypt, look..."

"My name is Blaze, mothafucka. Now, what does the FBI want with me and my family?" she asked while driving her knee into his thigh and digging her nails into his manhood that was still in her hand ever so slightly. Trey winced in pain, stifling any noise but getting the hint that Blaze would really fuck him up to get answers if need be.

"You took the files, so don't play stupid. You know what the FBI wants with your family, Blaze," he said, all but admitting to what she now knew was the truth.

"Fuck! I can't believe—fuck!" Blaze yelled. She looked down at Trey with fury in her eyes. Blaze released his shaft and quickly hit him with the handle of her pistol using all her strength. He fell sideways on the couch, away from her, in pain, with blood running down his face. In what seemed like one swift motion, Blaze jumped up and high-tailed it out the door.

Trey sat on his couch, holding the side of his face in his hands. He really fucked up. He had broken protocol from day one when he had taken things too far and fucked Blaze. Then, he let her into his place. After he crossed the line on the boat that night, he should have let his superiors know and been pulled from the case, but he kept his mouth shut because this woman had him hooked, literally in the blink of an eye. Trey played with fire and gotten burnt by falling for Blaze. He didn't know what he was going to do, but he knew shit just hit the fan, and it had to be fixed before it all blew up in his face.

CHAPTER 15
ANGEL

"I CAN RESPECT AN HONEST HOE. IT'S THE SNEAKY BITCHES THAT I DON'T LIKE."

Angel had been trying to spend a lot more time at the club lately. She could gather as much information that Trey could use as quickly as possible before she got caught and got herself into some serious trouble. She was sitting at the bar, checking her text messages when she spotted Black by the pool tables. He was alone, which rarely happened, so she jumped at the opportunity to have a conversation with him. Angel leaned over the bar, grabbed two Bud Lights in a bottle, and made her way over to where Black was standing.

"Hey. What's up?" she asked nervously.

"Oh uhh... Hey," Black responded with his eyebrows raised and a comical expression on his face, almost laughing at her.

"You want someone to play with?" Angel asked while motioning toward the closest pool table. She handed Black one of the Bud Lights she brought over.

"Do you actually know what you're doing?" he asked while taking a sip of his beer and looking at Angel with a side eye.

"Yeah. I've gotten pretty good since being here. I play every time I get a free moment, granted, I've only been playing against myself. I might can give you a run for your money, though," she replied, a bit flirtatiously.

"Right... rack 'em up then," he told her while walking over to grab two pool sticks from the wall. Black noticed Laila staring at them from behind the bar and laughed to himself. He shot her a sly smirk from across the room. She glared back before rolling her eyes a tad too noticeably and turning back around to continue working.

"Thanks for the beer, sweetheart. Angel, right?" he asked.

"Yeah. I didn't know you knew who I was, and you're welcome. You seem to be a big deal around here, being VP of the Kings and all, so I figured it would just be like common courtesy to come bearing gifts," she replied. Black laughed, more to himself, and took another sip of his beer. He watched as she put the balls into position on the table.

"So, what's your real name?" Angel asked.

"I mean, I know nobody uses real names around here, but I was just curious... you know... in the spirit of getting to know each other," she added.

"Just curious, huh? Well, my real name is Kareem, but I actually got my nickname from Blaze years ago. I was still a prospect back then... we were teenagers," he replied while looking into the distance. Angel could see the longing in his gaze. Just the mention of Blaze caused him to reminisce.

"Whenever we would talk, I was always telling her about African spirituality and culture because my parents were teaching me at the time. She always told me I was more than a regular Black man...I was extra Black or some corny shit like that, and the name kind of stuck," Black told her while still looking off in another direction and smiling to himself. He opened up his vest to reveal a small block of Kente cloth sewn over the top of his gun holster that was made into the vest.

"I never would have guessed that. I didn't realize y'all had known each other so long. Y'all got some serious history. Did you give Blaze her nickname too?" Angel asked.

"Nah. Her pops, Anthony, gave her that name not long after I got my real cut, but it was before I became vice president," he said while breaking the balls on the table and beginning the game.

"Everybody has a story, so what's the story behind her name?" Angel asked. Black paused mid hit and looked Angel up and down.

"Now that's something you'll have to ask her yourself. That's not my story to tell," Black told her as his stood up.

"But the fact that you're over here trying to squeeze me for some info on it tells me she already curved about that. Tread lightly, newbie," he whispered to her over her shoulder so she was the only one that heard. Black stepped around her while looking at her suspiciously, put down the pool stick, picked up his beer, and then walked away.

CHAPTER 16
LAILA

"WE CRAVE WHAT WE CAN'T HAVE."

Laila was at the club as usual and decided to do some inventory before they opened while she waited for Blaze. She received a call from Blaze about an hour ago letting her know she was going to have dinner with this new guy, Trey, and that she was going to invite him to come to the club later. Laila hoped Blaze didn't make a habit out of this because she didn't take too well to outsiders. That was already apparent by her attitude and distrust of Angel.

Laila was doing inventory and counting how much Corona was left behind the bar when she happened to look across the room and spot Angel. She noticed Angel talking to Black, and her demeanor was kittenish to say the least. Laila continued to watch as Angel handed Black a beer and continued to chat it up with him. Laila's gut feelings were on full red alert. Everything about the girl was all wrong, and she was going to figure out what it was. Black shot her a smirk from across the room, and she rolled her eyes before turning around and shaking her head. *This nigga probably thinks I was checking for him just now, with his arrogant ass*. At that exact moment, Roxy happened to be coming from the back with a case of Bud Light in her arms.

"I had no idea," Roxy said nonchalantly without even looking at Laila as she put the box on the bar top.

"What are you talking about?" Laila asked nervously.

"Girl, stop it. It's me... Roxy. You know you can tell me anything. I see things before people tell me. You already know this. Everybody in the club has secrets that are locked away with me. It's an unwritten rule. I'm like the house therapist, so spill it, mami," she said.

"I still don't know what you're talking about," Laila replied, trying, and failing, to play dumb. She picked her clipboard up and pretended to write on her inventory sheet, hoping Roxy would leave her alone. Instead, Roxy stepped closer to her and pulled the clipboard from her hand.

"You and Black... really?" Roxy asked in low tone so as to ensure Laila was the only one who could hear her. Laila averted her eyes, but Roxy continued to stare her down with a raised eyebrow.

"I'm going to fuck him up! What did he tell you?" Laila whispered. Roxy laughed out loud and went to her box to open it.

"He said... absolutely nothing, but you, my love, just told me everything I needed to know."

Laila shook her head and laughed, amused that she had fallen for the oldest trick in the book and had allowed Roxy to make her dry snitch on herself.

"I can't believe I fell for that. Nothing happened, though... not really. I mean... we were on that first weapons run, and we had to be in character."

Laila looked around to make sure nobody was listening in on their conversation.

"Look... we kissed because we were in character, but then we got a little *too* into character. Things got pretty hot between us, but I stopped it... that's all. It ain't like we fucked," Laila explained.

"Yeah. It ain't like y'all fucked... yet. You sound like you're not just trying to convince me but yourself, too, that it was just a kiss... in character. Baby girl, stop it. All I'm going to say is I don't judge. I, of all people, know that shit happens, but if you pursue that path, you better make sure that's one hundred percent what you want because there won't be any coming back from it. Black and Blaze got real deep history... real deep. It's almost like an other-worldly bond between them, even though they appear to hate each other's guts to outsiders. What I'm talking about has nothing to do with romance, either, and that's where it gets messy. They could both try to kill each other today, but their history and the things they've done—"

Roxy stopped herself so she wouldn't say too much because there was plenty that Laila didn't know about her bestie.

"Long story short, you're dealing with some dangerous territory. Those are lines you can't uncross. If I noticed it, that means other people can too. Just be sure of your feelings, and don't be thinking with just your kitty," Roxy said.

"It's not really that deep, Rox, so it's not going to turn into anything," Laila stated.

"Like I said, baby girl, you don't have to convince me. I would just hate to see something happen to you for some guy you're not sure about... especially when your relationship with your best friend is at stake," Roxy told her.

Laila was just about to deny having any type of feelings for Black again when Angel popped up out of nowhere on the other side of the bar.

"Shit! Can we get some bells on this bitch's ankles or something? Damn. You're always somewhere creeping. I really don't like that shit," Laila said to Angel.

"Hey to you, too, Laila. I didn't even come over here for you. I came to tell Roxy that there's a guy on the phone about a custom paint job with his kid's face or something that he wants put on his bike," Angel said. Roxy paused and put the beer she had in her hand back in the box.

"Yeah... okay. I'll take the call in the back office. Thanks, Angel," Roxy said, and she took off toward the club's office with her head down. Angel and Laila sized each other up for a few more seconds after Roxy left. Angel looked back over her shoulder at Black, and then she shot Laila a knowing smirk before she walked off.

As soon as Angel walked off, Laila's eyes lit up because she realized Angel left her phone on the counter. She looked around and saw that no one was paying her any attention. Laila scooped up that phone like it was a hundred-dollar bill and took off toward the changing room in the back.

CHAPTER 16
LAILA

"PEOPLE WILL STAB YOU IN THE BACK AND THEN ASK WHY YOU'RE BLEEDING."

Laila got inside the changing room and locked the door behind her. From the moment Laila laid eyes on Angel, she felt something wasn't right, but she could never seem to put her finger on what it was about her. Laila tapped the screen, and the phone opened. Angel left it unlocked.

"Stupid bitch," Laila said aloud to herself while shaking her head and going straight to the text messages. As soon as Laila opened Angel's texting app, her jaw dropped. She saw the name Trey with 234 messages locked inside. Trey was a common name, but honestly, what were the odds that this would be the same Trey Blaze was now seeing? Laila opened the messages and began to read through them, and her heart damn near jumped out of her chest.

Trey: where r u
Angel: at the club
Trey: u get info from Black
Angel: no, he got suspicious, wouldn't say anything about Blaze
Trey: need info fast, running out of time on the case

Laila almost threw the phone but decided against it. Instead, she picked up her own phone and was going to text Blaze 9-1-1. She was halfway through when she was grabbed from behind.

"Shhhhh!" said a voice from behind her. Laila turned around, and it was none other than Black. She started to back away from him, confused and unsure of what his intentions were. She was already on level ten because of what she had finally discovered about Angel. The last thing she needed was another incident with Black.

"What the fuck do you want, Black? Did you follow me back here on purpose?" Laila asked while slowly moving her hand toward the inside of her vest where her small revolver was hidden. Black had a hungry look in his eye, and quicker than she could blink, he grabbed Laila by her arm and pinned her to the nearest wall.

"Calm down," he whispered in her ear. He reached around the front of her, took the revolver from her hidden holster, and then released her.

"What do you want, Black?" Laila asked again while looking him up and down, pausing on his Herculean arms.

"You know what I want, Laila," he said with an added sultriness to his voice, taking a step closer to her.

"You want it too. You've wanted since that gun run we did together, but the only difference is that I'm not lying to myself about it," he said while taking yet another step closer. Laila was frozen and didn't know what to do.

"No… no, this is wrong. This is sooooo wrong," Laila said while taking a step back from Black.

"I saw you get a lil' jealous earlier. I saw you watching me from across the room, making sure I wasn't flirting with anyone," Black told her softly and seductively. At this point, he was inches from Laila, who hadn't taken another step away.

"There's this heat between us. Am I wrong?" Black asked while grabbing Laila by the back of her neck a bit aggressively.

"Yeah... yeah, there's something."

There was a slight quiver in Laila's voice when she spoke, a tell-tale sign that she didn't have much longer before she wouldn't be able to resist him anymore.

"We're not trying to fall in love. We're grown, and we're attracted to each other. Nobody has to know," Black said while reaching under her shirt with his other hand to caress her perky breasts.

"Hell yeah. It's nothing serious... we would just be fucking, right?" she asked while holding on to his muscles.

"Yeah, and what happens between us, stays between us. I know you can keep a secret," Black told her, reassuring her as he reached down to unbutton her denim jeans.

"But here? It's too risky," Laila said nervously while glancing in the direction of the door.

"We good. I've been wanting that little chocolate pussy for a long time. I want it now!" Black said with a subtle growl at the end. Laila hadn't even noticed he had gotten her pants and panties off while he'd been seducing her with his words.

Black lifted Laila into the air and on to his face with ease, cradling her thighs and supporting her body. Laila could tell already that Black was going to be a sexual show-off. There was no real reason to lift her the air to do what he was about to do, but she damn sure wasn't going to stop him.

"Wait—" Laila said as she reached up to touch the ceiling and steady herself. She was going to tell him to back up so she could steady herself on the wall but *wait* was the only word she managed to get out before Black started to devour her pearl. She closed her eyes and leaned her head back as she allowed him to work his magic. She felt his tongue go around and around her clit, faster and then slow, fast, and then slow again. He dipped his tongue into her pussy a few times and then started to slurp her on jewel with the tip of his juicy lips. It sounded like he was trying to suck the last bit of drink out of the bottom of a cup with a straw.

"Fuuuuuck, I'm about to cum! Ooooo, don't stop... don't stop," Laila moaned. Black began to work his tongue more furiously than ever. Once she started bucking against his face and rotating her hips feverishly, he knew he had her. Suddenly, he felt Laila's legs tremble.

"Hold up! Wait! Fuck! Black, I'm going to fall! Oooo, this shit feels so goooood," Laila said atop Black's shoulders. He squeezed her thighs with his strong hands as if to say *I got you*. Black locked in on her clit and started to make his tongue vibrate, and Laila couldn't hold it in any longer.

"Black, I'm cummin'... Oh my God!" Laila cried out as she started to cum, and she creamed all over Black's face. He let her down gently from his shoulders, and she reached up to kiss him, licking her own juices from his lips.

Laila reached down to undo Black's pants, and as she did that, he was about to take his vest off.

"Uh uh," Laila said while stopping him.

"Leave it on," she told him, and he gave her a devilish grin. Laila pulled out Black's black monster of a dick and swallowed it whole, taking its entire length into her mouth. Black tapped her on the head, unable to speak because of how good it felt.

"Bring yo' fine ass over here," he told her when she released him from her mouth, motioning to the extra-large mirror in the changing room.

"I want you to see what I see. I really noticed that bad ass lil' body you had in that outfit on the weapons run. Yeah... I saw you poke that ass out a lil' more every time you walked by me. I want you to see how fucking good you look while I'm diggin' all in that kitty," he told her. Black bent her over in front of the mirror and slapped her ass one good time. Laila turned to look in the mirror and watched as Black slid his dick in slowly, giving her body a chance to open up to him a bit more. He started off stroking her easy, and then he started to speed up. Laila grabbed on to her ankles, looking to the side and admiring how amazing their bodies actually looked together in the mirror.

"Hell yeah... that's it, Daddy! Get this pussy!" Laila told him. She released her ankles, put her hands on the wall, and started to throw her ass back, meeting every one of his thrusts.

"Damn, girl! Yeah... throw it back on me like that... there you go! What you trying to do to me!" Black shouted out. With all the moaning and shit talking that they were doing, it seemed as if the two forgot where they were and the severity of what was taking place. Moments later, they were most definitely reminded of the circumstances when the door burst open, and both of them nearly passed out.

CHAPTER 18
BLAZE

"AND THEN SUDDENLY, FOR NO APPARENT REASON, EVERYTHING STARTED TO FALL APART TOO QUICKLY TO FIX."

"You dog ass bitch!" Blaze screamed at the top of her lungs as soon as she burst through the door. Laila and Black tried to quickly grab their clothes, but Laila never got the chance to do so. Blaze tackled her to the ground and delivered blow after blow to her face and her body, whatever she could access. Laila struggled beneath her, trying to shield her own face, but Blaze had Laila pinned beneath her with her legs. Blaze grabbed Laila by the now messy and mangled long hair on her head and slammed it into the tiled floor with all her strength. She was two seconds from doing it again when she was immediately lifted into the air by Black.

"Let me explain, Egypt!" Black yelled while trying to hold Blaze at bay and keep her from beating Laila to death.

"No! Fuck you! You dirty mothafucka! Why choose my gahdamn best friend, Black? Huh?" Blaze yelled while still trying to escape Black's grip.

"Let me go, nigga! I'm about to kill that un-loyal hoe ass bitch and you too!" she yelled. Laila was on the floor groaning and holding her head, mainly from having her dome smashed.

There was blood everywhere from Blaze slamming Laila's head into the floor. By this time, Roxy appeared in the doorway to the changing room.

"Shit!" she said while running over to Laila on the floor and dropping to her knees beside her to help. Roxy looked up at Black, who was still restraining Blaze and then back down at Laila's naked bloody body. A look of horror fell across her face as the reality of what had gone down set in.

"What the fuck have y'all done?" Roxy said aloud, shaking her head. Roxy took off her Nubian Riders' vest and covered as much of Laila's bare body as she could.

"Let me go!" Blaze shouted furiously, and Black finally released her from his arms. Blaze reached in her vest a pulled out her nine-millimeter.

"Blaze, don't!" Roxy screamed while shielding Laila, knowing Blaze would never risk hurting her too.

"I'm not going to kill that bitch... yet. It would be a waste of a gahdamn bullet," Blaze said while laughing cynically. She removed the magazine from the gun, and in the blink of an eye, she busted Black in the face with the handle of her pistol. She spat at his feet and turned to leave the room. Reaching to grab the side of his head, which was now dripping blood, Black didn't say a word. He knew he deserved that and much more.

"The phone," Laila struggled to get out. Blaze stopped, and everyone turned to look at Laila.

"Angel's phone," Laila said while still holding her own head. She pointed to a phone sitting on a nearby countertop. Blaze glared at Laila menacingly, but she still walked over to grab the phone.

"The fuck does this have to do with anything?" Blaze

snapped with venom in her voice as she grabbed the phone from the floor.

"Just please... look at her messages," Laila managed to get out despite the excruciating pain she was experiencing. Blaze shook her head and went to the text messages in Angel's phone. She saw Trey's name, and she immediately felt her heart drop as her body shook with rage. With what she had walked in on a few moments ago, she had almost forgotten her whole reason for coming to the club, and it was the fact that she found out Trey wasn't who he claimed he was. Her original plan had been to call a meeting with the members that were present at the time, but now she had a whole different snake that she had to deal with.

Glancing at the phone that was in her hand, Blaze walked over to the entrance where she dropped the folder she inconspicuously snatched from Trey's place. She opened the folder and began reading. After a few seconds, Blaze turned and threw the phone at the wall, shattering it because everything was starting to make more sense.

"What now?" Black asked with an expression of confusion on his face. He looked back and forth between Laila, Roxy, and Blaze.

"Angel is a fucking FED!" Blaze shouted. With her nine-millimeter still at her side, she sprinted out of the room with Black following close behind. When Blaze got to the bar area, there were Nubian Riders mixed in with some of the Kings and their ol' ladies. Blaze spotted Angel back by the pool tables, and she went straight across the room at her. There were random shouts and gasps coming from all over the room as people noticed a blood splattered Blaze, gun in hand, headed straight toward Angel with a murderous look in her eyes.

Angel turned around and saw Blaze coming for her. She tried

to make a run for it but to no avail. Blaze cut her off in front of the bar, grabbing her by the throat. One of the King's ol' ladies screamed at the sight. Blaze put the gun in Angel's mouth, and Angel was visibly terrified.

"I'm only going to ask you once. Who the fuck are you?" Blaze asked in almost a whisper. Angel was breathing hard, and her eyes watered from the pistol that was practically being shoved down her throat. She tried to shake her head but couldn't, so she squeezed Blaze's arm to let her know she had something to say. With narrowed eyes, Blaze removed the gun from her mouth.

"I don't know what you—"

"Bitch! Don't insult my muthafuckin' intelligence!" Blaze shouted, shoving her pistol against Angel's forehead, causing her to jerk slightly.

"Who the fuck are you? Are you a fucking FED? Who sent you?" Blaze yelled, this time while tightening her grip around Angel's throat. Angel looked down and shook her head, which vexed Blaze. She was literally seconds away from killing the girl, and she had no explanation to give.

Shoving the gun back in Angel's mouth, Blaze told her, "You know what? There is really no explaining this shit. I read the messages between you and Trey. I don't care what your title is. You bitch ass law enforcement gon' learn not to come for me and my family, one way or the other."

Although the nine-millimeter was jammed back in Angel's mouth, it was still crystal clear that a devilish smile was trying to creep across Angel's face. Cocking her head to the side and caught off guard by Angel's demeanor, Blaze removed the gun but still had it trained on Angel's skull. Coughing a bit, Angel looked Blaze straight in the eyes as she responded.

"I'm no FED, baby," Angel replied in an eerily calm way that was an extreme contrast to how terrified she had just been moments ago. Everyone in the room was noticeably confused.

"Does the name Dominic Ruiz ring any bells for you?" Angel asked while looking in Blaze's eyes, searching for an answer in them. Blaze looked back at Black, and both of them looked back at Angel, mutually horrified and a tad fearful, as if they had just seen a ghost.

"There's no fuckin' way..." Blaze started to say while shaking her head and looking Angel up and down for what felt like the first time. Blaze never thought the day would come, but there she was, literally looking her past right in its eyes. At that moment, Angel felt Blaze's grip relax ever so slightly from around her throat, and she seized the opportunity in that moment. Angel brought her knee up to Blaze's stomach, knocking the wind out of her. Before anyone could react, Angel had drawn her pistol and had it pointed at Blaze. At this point, everyone inside the club was staring at them, on edge, watching the scene play out as if watching a drama on television.

"Just clear a path," Angel commanded while walking toward Blaze.

"Everybody just chill," Blaze said aloud while backing up toward the entrance of the club, holding Angel's gaze the entire way there. The two of them got all the way to the door without issue.

"Outside!" Angel roared at Blaze.

"That shit ain't about to go down!" Black yelled, coming straight for Angel.

"Uh uh uh..." Angel said as she cocked the hammer on the gun and pressed it against the center of Blaze's forehead. Black stopped dead in his tracks, not knowing what to do next.

"You want me outside? I'll go the fuck outside," Blaze told her fiercely.

"If any one of you mothafuckas follow, she's dead!" Angel shouted through the club.

"I got it, y'all," Blaze said, still keeping her composure and displaying her most convincing poker face, although she felt like she was about to shit bricks. Angel backed Blaze out the door and waited until the door completely shut before she began speaking again.

"The score we have to settle is just between me and you. Don't think that because you're still standing I'm going to have mercy on you. I just know if I kill you now, I won't even make it to the highway alive without everyone inside that club over there trying to put a bullet in me, but know this..." Angel said, taking a step closer and ramming the barrel of her gun into the side of Blaze's cheek.

"...I swear on my father's grave that you, your father, and your ex-partner-in-crime, Black, are going to pay for my father's death all those years ago. When I start picking y'all off one by one, your friends and families will chalk it up to freak accidents or bad luck... but you'll know better. Deep down, you'll know exactly who it was and why it's happening because I'll save you for last, baby girl," Angel said, blowing a kiss at Blaze.

Angel turned away from Blaze, pointed her gun in the opposite direction, and fired, seemingly to clear her chamber. She hopped on her motorcycle and sped off. Blaze exhaled and ran her hands down her face, giving her heart a moment to calm down as it had been about to beat out of her chest during this whole ordeal. Looking around, still a bit in shock, she realized Angel shot out one of the tires on her bike.

Black came bursting outside with gun in hand after hearing

the shot go off. He saw Blaze standing there, looking off in the direction Angel fled, and he lowered his piece.

"What did she say?" Black asked. He looked over at Blaze's motorcycle, which was now sitting on a flat.

"Laila was right all along," Blaze said, not really to Black but mostly to herself. She looked over at Black, pushed him out of her way, and walked back in the club as her anger toward him and Laila that had been momentarily forgotten came back to the forefront. All eyes were on Blaze when she walked back in the club. Everyone was watching and waiting to see what her next move was going to be. She immediately spotted Roxy emerging from the changing room helping Laila who was back dressed and trying not to draw attention to herself. At this point, Blaze didn't care about making a scene or everyone knowing what was going on. Making her way across the room, she stopped in front of Roxy and Laila, who wouldn't even look her the eye.

"Take off my gahdamn vest... and get the fuck out my bar," Blaze said with a venomous calmness in her voice. All across the room people were muttering to each other and trying to figure out what was going on. Laila took off her vest and handed it over. Blaze grabbed it and allowed it to fall to the floor before taking off in the direction of her office and closing the door on all the madness that just happened.

CHAPTER 19
DEONTRE

"NO TURNING BACK... NO REGRETS."

Deontre was in the kitchen icing his face. He royally fucked up and was trying his best to figure out what his next move was going to be. He looked down at his phone to check his messages. He tried to text Angel several times, telling her that it was all over and to get out while it was still safe to do so. She wasn't responding, and all he could do was hope for the best but prepare for the worst.

Suddenly, his other phone rang, and he knew it had to be the bureau. He stared over at it, not knowing what to do. He had done everything wrong, and if things didn't go in his favor after he explained his mistakes to his superiors, he could get fired and possibly face prison time. He stood in his kitchen, frozen, holding the ice pack to his face where Blaze had knocked him with her gun, and waiting on his cell phone's voicemail to pick up the call.

Trey began to pace back and forth, and suddenly, he knew he only had one option. He ran to his hall closet, grabbed a suitcase, and began to pack. His phone continued to ring off the hook as he went through his house grabbing anything important that he could, his personal guns, all the cash from his safe, and some clothes. Trey's phone began to ring again. He glanced at it for a moment, conflicted on what he should do until finally he answered.

"This is Agent Daniels," he answered.

"We need you to report in. Due to an essential piece of evidence, we got the warrant for Egypt's club, Leather and Lace, from Judge Stewart. Everyone is gearing up to go in, and we need you here before we make that move," the voice replied back.

"Yes, sir. I'm just leaving my mother's house in the country. I'm about an hour and a half out. I'll be there as soon as I can, sir," Trey told him.

"Alright... and Agent Daniels? Great work, son!" the voice said with authority.

"Thank you, sir," Trey said before hanging up. Exhaling, Trey set his suitcase by the door and went to grab his other phone, his personal phone. He reached up to grab a large bowl from his cabinet and filled it with hot water. After throwing both the phones on the floor and successfully shattering them, he took the phones apart and put them both in the bowl of water.

Trey made his way to the door and grabbed his suitcase, about to leave. When he turned around to glance back at his apartment one last time, he looked on his kitchen table and spotted the Tiffany's box still in place from the dinner date that was supposed to go down with Blaze before everything had blown up in his face. Looking back, he had no idea how he'd gotten to this point of chaos so quickly, but from the first time he'd laid his eyes on Blaze, she had him under her spell. He originally planned to give Blaze the gift in an effort to show her that she had no reason to regret their episode on the boat. He wanted to make it known that she was more than a piece of pussy to him.

He stared at the box for a second with hope, then grabbed it and left, slamming the door shut on his old life for good.

CHAPTER 20
BLAZE

"LIFE IS LIKE A BOOMERANG..."

Blaze was in her office at the club, pacing back and forth. She didn't know if she wanted to cry or to kill someone. Emotionally, she was all over the place, and she was definitely having a hard time processing everything that had just happened to her in a short period of time. First, she found out that the man she had been falling for was working for the FBI and had been investigating her. Then, not only had she found out that her best friend was fucking her ex-fiancé, but she had done so by walking in on them in the act. If anything else major happened that day, she felt that she just might lose it, and then her phone rang. Blaze looked at her phone, and all it said was *unavailable*. Despite what she felt was the smart thing to do, her gut instinct told her to answer the call.

"Don't hang up!" the voice yelled as soon as she picked up. She immediately recognized the voice, and it was apparently Trey calling her from another number.

"What the fuck do you want, Trey? We have nothing else to talk about, you snake ass mothafucka! You were using me," Blaze said with pain in her voice.

"Look, I know you're hurt, and part of you probably wants to kill me for lying to you, but we don't have time for that right now. You have got to listen to me, Blaze," Trey said to her. Blaze wanted so badly to curse him out, hang up the phone, and be done with him, but there was a sense of urgency in his tone when he spoke.

"Do you trust me?" Trey asked. Blaze's mind went back to their first date. She started to reminisce about the time they had spent together and the way that he had made love to her. Blaze quickly shook those thoughts away.

"I don't have time for your bullshit ass, stupid ass questions. You know good and gahdamn well I can't trust you as far as I can throw you. Say whatever the fuck you've got to say, nigga, before I hang up. I got a lot going on right now," Blaze shot back at him.

"You're right. I'm sorry for that. Where are you right now?" he asked.

"You don't need to know that, Trey. I'm about to hang up on your ass if you don't tell me what is so important. What, nigga?" she yelled into the phone.

"If you're at Leather and Lace, you need to leave now. I got a call about ten minutes ago from the bureau. They found something, Blaze. I don't know what it is, but it's some kind of concrete evidence that got them the warrant they needed. They're coming for the club with guns locked and loaded," he said, running most of his words together.

"What?... What did they...Why are you telling me this? You're the one who has been investigating me and trying to get me caught up. Why the fuck should I believe you? This could be a last-minute trick to get me to walk out of my club and right into a trap," she asked him. The FEDS were coming, and her pulse started to race all over again. If she wasn't careful, her young heart would give out from all the things she'd been through in one day. Blaze didn't know if she could handle this right now on top of everything else.

"You can't see it now, but I'm trying to protect you, baby. I stopped giving the FEDS real tips to go on the day I realized I was falling for you. I've been feeding them a bunch of bogus ass information damn near since the beginning. You have a snitch in your club who is feeding them the real shit," Trey said.

"You're unbelievable. I know I had a snitch in my club. It was your little rat, Angel. Yeah. We just figured her out," Blaze said while her anger was steadily rising back up.

"No, Blaze. Listen! It's not Angel. Somebody who knows what really happened that day sixteen years ago is on *their* side."

Blaze's eyes looked off into the distance. She hung up the phone on Trey and ran to the head of the table in her office. Blaze reached under the table and pressed the emergency button. All of a sudden, a loud siren, similar to a fire alarm, started to go off, and lights began to flash. Running out of the office to the bar area, she saw club members and their guests scrambling everywhere. A few people already dipped because she could hear motorcycles revving up outside and riding away.

She quickly made her way to the changing room in the back of her club. When she stepped in, she momentarily paused at the sight of Laila's blood that still stained the tiled floor. She quickly snapped back to reality and went in search of Roxy's locker. There was only one piece of evidence left in the world that could convict Blaze, and it was in Roxy's toolbox. She spotted Roxy's locker, riddled with her infamous graffiti, and was just about to pop it open when she heard hysterical screaming coming from outside. There were a few moments of silence and then a loud crash as the door to the changing room flew open.

"Freeze! Don't move! Put your hands where we can see them, Egypt!" a voice yelled. Blaze stopped in her tracks to see that five SWAT members had broken down the door, and they all had assault rifles aimed directly at her. While holding her hands high up in the air, Blaze slowly backed away from the locker and toward the men.

"Fuck!" she yelled. The only thing that stood between her and her freedom was right inside that locker, but she had been too little too late. One of the men stepped forward and handcuffed her. The one who had told her to freeze began walking toward the lockers. If he opened Roxy's locker, then her whole life was over. To Blaze's surprise, the man didn't go for Roxy's locker. He pulled a paper from his pocket, looked over it, and then went straight for Blaze's locker. She had no idea what the fuck was about to happen.

CHAPTER 21
DEONTRE

"I GOT YOU. 'LONG AS YOU GOT ME."

Trey knew he had to think fast. Once he had gotten in his car, he knew he had to warn Blaze in some type of way that her bar was about to be raided. He pulled over to the first gas station he came to and purchased a cellphone with cash. He went back to his Hummer and pulled out of the parking lot while calling Blaze. The phone rang a few times before she actually picked up.

"Don't hang up!" Trey yelled as soon as he heard the call connect. He blocked his number for Blaze's protection and had half expected her not to even pick up.

"What the fuck do you want, Trey? We have nothing else to talk about, you snake ass mothafucka! You were using me," Blaze said. She was angry but clearly trying to mask her hurt at the same time.

"Look, I know you're hurt, and part of you probably wants to kill me for lying to you, but we don't have time for that right now. You have got to listen to me, Blaze," Trey said to her. Telling her the information about the raid could compromise everything he worked so hard for in his career his entire life, but the woman that was stealing his heart was in trouble, and he felt he didn't have a choice.

"Do you trust me?" Trey asked. There was a silence on the line, which gave Trey a second to realize how stupid he sounded asking that question now that Blaze knew the truth about who he was. Of course, her answer would be no.

"I don't have time for your bullshit ass, stupid ass questions. You know good and gahdamn well I can't trust you as far as I can throw you. Say whatever the fuck you've got to say nigga, before I hang up. I got a lot going on right now," Blaze shot back at him.

"You're right. I'm sorry for that. Where are you right now?" he asked. He prayed deep down that she didn't say the club.

"You don't need to know that, Trey. I'm about to hang up on your ass if you don't tell me what is so important. What, nigga?" she yelled into the phone.

"If you're at Leather and Lace, you need to leave now. I got a call about ten minutes ago from the bureau. They found something, Blaze. I don't know what it is, but it's some kind of concrete evidence. They're coming for the club with guns locked and loaded," he said, running most of his words together. He figured that by her not wanting to say where she was that she was, indeed, at the club.

"What? What did they...Why are you telling me this? You're the one who has been investigating me and trying to get me caught up. Why the fuck should I believe you? This could be another one of your bullshit tricks to get me to walk out of my club and right into a trap," she asked him.

"You can't see it now, but I'm trying to protect you, baby. I stopped giving the FEDS real tips to go on the day I realized I was falling for you. I've been feeding them a bunch of bogus ass information for a while now. You have a snitch in your club who is feeding them the real shit," Trey told her. It seemed that she was too clouded by her anger toward him to be able to comprehend how much trouble was coming her way.

"You're unbelievable. I know I had a snitch in my club. Your little rat, Angel. Yeah. We figured her out," Blaze said. It immediately hit him that she figured out Angel was a plant for him inside her club, but she was still wrong.

"No, Blaze. Listen! It's not Angel. Somebody who knows what really happened that day sixteen years ago is on *their* side," Trey said. There was a momentary silence, and then the call ended. Blaze had hung up, and Trey knew he had to intervene, or Blaze's life was over. Trey hit the accelerator and sped off toward Blaze's club.

Trey knew the rendezvous point for the SWAT team and the officers would be about five minutes away from the club, so he kept his eyes peeled the closer he got. Finally, he spotted the team in the parking lot of a closed down gas station. He figured he would only have one chance to pull this off, so he had to make it count.

Trey pulled into the lot and parked. He took a few deep breaths to calm his nerves before stepping out of his Hummer and walking over to where his superior officer was standing, waiting for him.

"Man of the hour! Here he is!" his boss shouted.

"I thought you wouldn't make it in time," his boss added, walking toward the trunk of one of the jeeps that was also parked there. He popped it open to reveal Trey's tactical gear waiting for him. Trey began suiting up, and his adrenaline started pumping.

"Alright... we're moving out. Let's make this quick and clean, folks!" his boss yelled to the crew. They loaded up and made their way toward the club. Trey just bowed his head, praying that his plan would work.

Pulling up to the club, they could all see people running out, and a loud siren-like noise could be heard.

"Move! Move! Move!" the boss shouted. Trey could hear screams as the men entered. He went inside last.

"Shit!" he said to himself. He didn't know where the hell Blaze was, but the window of time she had to escape was closing fast. His eyes suddenly shifted to the back of the club, and he saw the remnants of a busted down door. Trey ran full speed in the direction of the changing room and stopped right before he went in. He took a second to collect himself and walked in with his shoulders back and chin up. He immediately saw Blaze in handcuffs, and one of the SWAT team members was heading to a specific locker.

"I'll go ahead and take Egypt in for questioning and booking," Trey said aloud. The man holding on to Blaze nodded. At the sound of his voice, Blaze whipped around quickly, and a look of utter confusion fell over her face. Trey looked into her eyes intensely and tried to have a silent conversation with her, letting her know that he was on her side. Apparently, she got the hint and began to play along.

"I'm not going anywhere with that mothafucka!" she yelled as she spit in his direction. The officer who cuffed her hit her with an elbow to the gut, using all of his strength. Blaze cried out in pain and doubled over while coughing. Trey clenched his jaw hard. It took everything in him not to beat the man in the head with his rifle for even laying a finger on Blaze, but he had no choice but to hold it together.

"Here! Take her!" the man said to Trey.

"I'll head over to the station with her now. Call me as soon as you find something so I know for sure what I've got to work with," Trey commanded.

"Yes, sir," the other man said. The other four men nodded in agreement, and Trey snatched Blaze by the arm, hightailing it to the front door. Still in handcuffs, Blaze looked up at Trey with desperation in her eyes. He kept his eyes forward and gave her arm an extra tight squeeze, letting her know not to blow their cover. Right before they walked out the door of the club, Trey glanced back quickly to make sure no one was following them or paying them any attention. He happened to see Roxy handcuffed by the bar. When she spotted him, her eyes grew to twice their normal size, and Trey pulled Blaze quickly through the door.

He routinely put Blaze in the back of one of the jeeps, and she looked longingly back at her motorcycle. Trey got in the driver seat, shut the door, and sped off in the direction of the abandoned gas station where he left his Hummer.

"Trey—" Blaze shouted, but he quickly cut her off. He pointed at the radio in the Jeep, and she sat back restlessly, understanding that it wasn't wise to talk at the moment. The tires screeched to a halt once they pulled up to the parking lot where Trey left his Hummer. He got out, went to the back seat, and opened the door. Blaze was itching to speak but knew there was a strong possibility of there being recording equipment in the jeep.

Trey took off Blaze's handcuffs and unlocked his Hummer, motioning for her to go ahead and get in it. He stripped off his tactical gear in less than a minute. Picking up his bulletproof vest, he decided that it may come in handy, so he chucked it into his Hummer. Going to the back of the jeep, he grabbed another bulletproof vest and the extra guns and ammo that his superior officer stashed there. Trey hurriedly jumped in the Hummer and took off in the direction of the highway.

For what seemed like forever, Blaze sat staring at him in shock.

"What... the... fuck?" she finally managed to say.

"What just happened, Trey? Better yet, where are you taking me?" she asked, turning her entire body in the seat to face him.

"You really feel like you have the right to question me right now? Do you know what the fuck I just did for you back there?" Trey yelled while looking back and forth between Blaze and the road. She noticed the veins at his temple and on the side of his neck bulge and pop out as he shouted.

"I didn't ask you to do a mothafuckin' thing for me, nigga. Who do you think you're talking to? All this is happening *because of you!*" Blaze yelled back. Trey started to laugh like an insane person, and it seemed to catch Blaze completely off guard.

"My fault?... My fault?... You killed someone in cold blood when you were only nineteen years old, but when the FBI finally begins its investigation on you, then it's my fault? You're unbelievable, ma. I just risked my own life and freedom so maybe we could start over and make some kind of life together, and you want to play the blame game? Un-fucking-believable," Trey told her, shaking his head, and keeping his eyes locked on the road ahead.

"So... what... we're going to run away together? Are we moving to Mexico or going to an island? How are we getting there, Trey? Are we going by plane? What about passports? You're acting like I'm supposed to be falling down to my knees to suck your dick as thanks to you for saving me so that we could disappear with each other, but did you actually think any of this through? Hell, what about my motorcycle? My bike is my life, nigga," Blaze said, going on and on. Trey couldn't take it anymore. His instincts took over, and he knew what he had to do. As illogical as it seemed at the moment, he pulled over to the side of the road and stopped the Hummer.

"Oh, so now what? I'm getting on your nerves already, so you're going to leave me out here by the side of the road for all your little FBI friends to come scoop me up?" Blaze asked as she continued to go in on him. Trey got out of the Hummer and made his way to Blaze's side all while he could still hear her rambling. She saw him coming for her and didn't know what was about to happen, so she tried to quickly lock the door. Apparently, she hadn't been fast enough.

Trey wrenched the door open as she tried to make it to the last row of seats by climbing over. Blaze didn't know what was going on, but she saw a hunger in his eyes. Trey didn't know what was going on in his own head. Maybe it was the adrenaline pumping through his body from everything that had happened in the past few hours coupled with Blaze's nagging, but his dick had begun to rise when Blaze was yelling at him, and he was about to give her some act right to fix her attitude, SWAT team be damned.

Trey grabbed her by the leg and forcefully brought her body closer to his, grabbing the back of her head and pulling her in for a kiss. He felt some of the tension leave Blaze's body when she realized what was happening and that she wasn't in danger. He broke the kiss first and pushed her back slightly. He undid her pants and snatched them down to her ankles. Blaze still had on her riding boots, so he couldn't get her pants all the way off.

"Trey, what the fuck is wrong with you? We don't have time for this! Have you lost your mind?"

"Fuck it," he said aloud. He unbuckled his own pants and

pulled his already rock-hard dick out of his boxers. Blaze was staring at him with a mixture of desire and fear in her expression that he had never seen before, and it turned him on even more. She kicked her boots off and pulled her pants from around her ankles. She slid off the seat in order to get down and give Trey some head, but he picked her up before she could and put her back in the passenger seat. Trey squatted down in front of her and placed her legs on his shoulders. He inhaled and exhaled deeply while just admiring her plump pink pussy for a moment, using his fingers to caress her lips a bit and admire how soft they were. Just the feeling of his breath on her throbbing lips down below made her body shudder.

Trey put two fingers to Blaze's mouth, and almost instantly, she licked them as if she were licking the bulging head of his dick. His reached down and stuck those two fingers into her pussy, curving them to reach her G-spot as he started eating her out. His tongue massaged every inch of her from her ass all the way to her clit. Trey began flicking his tongue on it quickly and Blaze's breathing sped up and became more audible. Trey got faster, and Blaze let her moans pour out just like the sweet nectar from her center was.

"Damn, Daddy! Yessssss! Right there! Don't stop! Ooooou, yes! That's it! Right there!" she shouted. Trey knew he had her good and that it would only be moments before she reached her climax because she grabbed his head with one hand and started to fuck his face.

"Shit, Trey! I'm about to cum! Oh my God! I'm about to cum!" Blaze screamed. Not even a second later, Trey felt her juices run down his chin. He quickly hopped up and penetrated her steadily pulsating pussy.

"Fuuuck," Trey said under his breath. Blaze's pussy was

already amazing, but as soon as he slid his manhood in, he felt her walls squeezing him tightly and pulling him in as she was still feeling the lingering effects from the orgasm she just had. He tilted his head back in ecstasy. He began to fuck her hard and fast, knowing they both needed this. Trey needed to relieve some stress, and she needed her attitude checked by the man who had just saved her from a jail cell for the time being.

Trey could hear how wet she was with every single one of his strokes. He kept hitting the pussy with the same rhythmic stroke, and it was as if he was really trying to blow her back out this time around. Trey continued to pound her harder into the seat of his car until he felt the sensation and knew he was almost at his peak.

"That's it, Trey! Come on, Daddy!" Blaze said from beneath him. It had never really been his thing but hearing her call him Daddy again drove him crazy.

"This pussy is too good! Fuck... fuck... fuck!" Trey shouted. He had held back long enough, so he let his body succumb to Blaze, and he came inside her. It seemed that once they had gotten their rocks off, they both snapped back to reality at the same moment, realizing how close they probably were to being caught.

"Hop in the back, baby. You can clean up there. We gotta go!" Trey told her. Trey quickly pulled up his pants, shut the passenger door, and Blaze crawled to the back seat. He ran around, hopped in the driver's seat, and sped off toward the highway again. Blaze popped up behind his shoulder and kissed him on the cheek.

"That's more like it," he said while smiling to himself.

"I can't believe you did that, Trey, but we have to get rid of this Hummer. I know how much you probably love it, but it's too noticeable. We need to get far away until we can get out of the country or something, too. Matter of fact, let me see the little burner you used to call me. We're going to need some help," Blaze said while zipping up her pants and reaching her hand up to the front seat. Trey handed her the little off-brand phone, and she grabbed it to make the call. The phone started ringing, and Blaze set it down on the arm rest and put it on speaker so she could put her boots back on.

"Hello?" Anthony said as his loud deep voice echoed throughout the Hummer.

"Pop, it's me!" Blaze said.

"What the fuck is happening, baby girl? I've been getting call after call about a whole bunch of shit that's going down. You damn near killed Laila! Is that true? I was told there was a raid on the club and that you were arrested. I don't know what's true and what's not!" Anthony said.

"I'm good. It's true... all of it, but I got away," she told him quickly. Blaze knew her father was crazy enough to go to the county jail and shoot everyone there to break her out if he thought she was locked up. She had to defuse his anger to keep him from taking drastic measures.

"How did you get out of there? I'm coming to you. Where are you?" he asked.

"I'll explain everything real soon, Pops. Do you remember that motel you went to that time you and Black had to dip out because of that bullshit ass warrant?" she asked, trying to trigger her father's memory.

"Yeah. I remember, baby girl," he replied.

"Meet me there when the sun goes all the way down. Bring a car that blends in. I need to switch out the one I'm in, and I need it disappeared... maybe a chop shop really far away," she told him. Trey turned to look back at her with a face that said fuck no. She motioned for him to turn around and keep driving.

"Okay. I can definitely do that. I'll see you soon," he said.

"Wait, Pops! Bring me some clothes and toiletries and stuff too. Use the money from my stash at your house. You can't get caught going to my place."

"Word. I've got you, sweetheart," Anthony said. Blaze hung up with her dad, feeling slightly relieved.

"Watch your arm, babe," Blaze said while tapping Trey on the shoulder. He shifted his body slightly, and she crawled up into the passenger seat.

"Why didn't you tell him I was going to be with you? He might not be cool with that, especially if he found out that I'm a FED... *was* a FED," Trey said, shaking his head. He was thinking about how the career he had worked for his whole life was now over in a flash.

"I have to hit him with a little bit of news at a time. My father is shot out a little bit and has been known to overreact sometimes. They used to call him Hulk for a good reason, and there's no *if* he finds out you were FED. I have to tell him because I don't keep secrets from that man... usually. I just have to figure out how to tell him," Blaze said while looking off away from Trey. "

We're going to this motel that's a couple hours away. I'll tell you how to get there. Just get on the highway and drive," Blaze told him. She grabbed Trey's hand, lacing her fingers between his. He picked her hand up and kissed the back of it as they merged on the highway, leaving their old lives behind them for good.

CHAPTER 22
BLAZE

"FATHER KNOWS BEST."

When Blaze and Trey reached the motel, he pulled the Hummer around the back, away from the view of passing cars. Blaze waited in the car while Trey walked around the side of the building and headed toward the office. She kept looking over her shoulder, out the back window, and at every other car in the parking lot. She picked up Trey's burner phone and decided to shoot her father a text.

Blaze: it's baby girl, we at the spot safe
Anthony: ok sweetheart, give me another hour
Blaze: k, I love you!
Anthony: wait, who is WE?
Blaze: ???????
Anthony: u said "we" at the spot

Blaze scrolled up to her earlier text messages and shook her head. *Damn*, she thought. She had definitely slipped up. She decided that for now, she would just play it off and ignore her father's question.

Blaze*: txt u wit room number soon, look for a Hummer in back parking lot*

She put the phone down just as she saw Trey coming back toward her.

"My pops will be here in about an hour. We should probably freshen up while we wait for him," Blaze said, hinting at the fact that they'd had sex on the side of the road and hadn't showered yet. She didn't want to smell like sex when her father showed up.

One hour later...

Trey's phone vibrated, and Blaze reached over to grab it. There was a text message from Anthony.

Anthony*: ROOM #!!!!!!!!*

"Shit!" Blaze said out loud.

"What's wrong, baby?" Trey asked from the bathroom.

"It's nothing major. I forgot to text my pops the room number earlier. Oh, and hurry up and put some clothes on. I already have no idea how he's going to react when I tell him who you are. If you're half naked when he gets here, it's only going to make things worse," she said.

"Yeah. You've got a point," he replied while putting on some sweatpants and a T-shirt from the bag he'd packed from his place. Blaze texted Anthony back to let him know that they were in room 227. Less than ten minutes later, there was a knock on the motel room door. Blaze grabbed her vest and took out the nine-millimeter that was hidden inside. She glanced at herself when she walked past the mirror. She tried to tidy up her extra-large clothes. After her shower, she remembered that she had only come with the clothes on her back. She had to put on a pair of Trey's sweats and a T-shirt until her father arrived with some of her things.

There was a knock at the door again. Blaze glanced through the peephole before opening the door for her father.

"It's so good to see you safe and sound! Do you know you're practically a legend in the streets now? You were taken into custody, and then you disappeared like damn Houdini. I knew you were good, baby girl, but no one has ever been *that* good. How the hell did you pull that off?" Anthony asked. At that exact moment, Trey came out the bathroom, clearing his throat.

"Hi, sir. I'm Deontre," Trey said. He stuck his hand out in order to shake hands with Anthony, but Anthony just stood there mean mugging him.

"Blaze... who the hell is this, and what the fuck does he have to do with all of this that's going on?" her father asked.

"Pops, this is Trey, and he helped me get away today," Blaze said while looking back and forth between Trey's outstretched hand and her father's intimidating stance. Anthony extended his hand to shake Trey's, but he still had a skeptical expression on his face.

"How long have you two known each other? Blaze has never mentioned you," Anthony said while cutting his eyes at his daughter. Trey looked at Blaze, and she gave him back a nervous look that said go ahead.

"We met about a week ago. I asked Blaze out, and she accepted. I uhh..." Trey said, trailing off. He looked over at Blaze, and she looked as if she were about to pass out.

"...I originally met your daughter because I had to... I was the lead investigator in—"

Pow! Trey was interrupted mid-sentence because the moment Anthony heard investigator, he clocked Trey right in the jaw.

"Pops!" Blaze shouted, going over to Trey.

"I'm fine, baby," Trey said. The sound of Anthony cocking his pistol caused both Blaze and Trey to turn and look at him.

"*Baby?*" Anthony asked, visibly livid and confused. He had his gun pointed directly at Trey, so Blaze stepped between the two of them.

"Who the hell is he, Blaze?" Anthony asked.

"Pops—"

"Nah, baby girl. I want to hear him say it out loud," Anthony said.

"It's okay, Blaze," Trey said. He turned to look Anthony in the eye.

"I have to ask you to put the heat down first, Mr. Johnson," Trey instructed in the calmest voice he could muster. Anthony looked back and forth between Trey and Blaze who had a look that was pleading for him to comply. Anthony allowed his arm to drop.

"You've got sixty seconds, nigga," Anthony told him.

"Sir... I'm Agent Daniels with the FBI, and I was put on a cold case where you, your daughter, and her ex-fiancé are all suspects. But..." Trey said as he took a step back. Anthony had fire in his eyes at this point.

"...I fell in love with your daughter damn near overnight, so I started feeding my superiors bullshit leads and false information to get them off her trail," Trey continued.

"If you were giving them a bunch of bullshit, why was my daughter's bar raided earlier today? There's no way a bunch of bullshit still brought them to the right place," Anthony said.

By his expression, Blaze could see the wheels turning in his head.

"They knew where to come because there is a snitch in Blaze's motorcycle club who has been giving them the real information. They came in the bar and knew exactly where to go... exactly which locker to go to for the murder weapon," Trey said. Anthony took a step forward while pushing Blaze to the side. He got right in Trey's face.

"Now how the fuck do I know you're not lying to me now? You could be the inside snitch but just be really good at lying to my daughter. She's protecting you from catching a hot one from me, so I know you have her nose wide open," Anthony said.

"He doesn't know anything," Blaze said, speaking up for Trey.

"It couldn't have been him because the only thing that he knows is from the file they already had," she continued. Anthony slackened his grip on the gun while shifting his eyes to the ground.

"None of this makes any sense," Anthony said aloud, more to himself than to anyone else in the room. Blaze took a step toward her father and placed both of her hands on the gun he was still holding. He looked up at her and allowed her to take the pistol from him. Blaze set it down on the bed as Trey exhaled the breath that he had been holding in.

"I know it doesn't make sense. It seems if we can find out who the real snitch is, we can begin to sort things out and do what we need to do to protect ourselves. I just don't know who would betray me... betray us like that. It couldn't be Roxy because she's as loyal as they come..."

When Blaze said this, Trey noticed Anthony's eyes become shifty. Anthony looked up with an expression that he had been caught doing something he shouldn't have been doing. The eyes were the gateway to the soul, and Anthony's eyes said that he was hiding something. Blaze was in deep thought and didn't notice the non-verbal exchange between the two men.

"...and Laila doesn't know much of anything. At least, she didn't know much of anything, but after finding out what I found out today, Laila being the snitch would make the most sense," Blaze said. The image of Laila bent over in front of the club's changing room mirror while Black power-drove her with his dick flashed through her head. She came to the conclusion right then and there that this affair between her ex-best friend and her ex-fiancé must have been going on for a long time. Maybe she was the mystery bitch Black had been cheating on her with the entire time they were together. Black must have gotten too comfortable and told Laila the story of what went down all those years ago.

Trey looked at Blaze with a confused expression. He could tell she had come to some type of realization in her mind.

"What did you find out today?" Trey asked. Blaze didn't respond immediately. She didn't want to let him know she had literally caught Laila and Black with their pants down and flipped out. If she told him everything that happened earlier today, he may think she still had feelings for Black, but she didn't. Her anger stemmed from the fact that she and Laila had been best friends since they were children. She just never thought that level of betrayal was possible from her right-hand chick.

"Nothing, baby," she finally replied.

"I just found out she isn't loyal like I thought she was. Laila is definitely the snitch," Blaze said conclusively to her father.

"Well then... you know what needs to be done," Anthony told her.

"I know exactly what needs to be done, and I want to be the one to do it. It's the only way," Blaze said. Trey just stood there, mildly in shock. He had no idea what all had transpired that day, but he knew he had definitely just listened to Blaze and Anthony give the greenlight on Laila's head.

"Trey, I've got some things for Blaze out in the car. Can you help me get them inside the room?" Anthony asked, turning to face Trey. Trey looked at the man like he had lost his damn mind. Not even five minutes prior, Anthony had pointed a gun to Trey's dome and probably would have killed him without thinking twice if it wasn't for Blaze. Now he was asking Trey to help him outside... alone.

Blaze looked at her father, realizing he probably just wanted to speak with him alone. She looked at Trey and saw him adjust his shirt. Blaze realized that Trey had probably been in the bathroom securing a gun in his waistband, just in case she hadn't been able to reason with her father after letting him know Trey was a FED. As crazy as the situation seemed, Blaze smirked to herself thinking about it. It almost turned her on to see Trey do something so sneaky.

"Go ahead. I'll be right here figuring out how we gon' get some food," Blaze said. The two men nodded in agreement and stepped out the door into the motel's parking lot.

CHAPTER 23

DEONTRE

"IN THIS NEW LIFE, I PREFER DANGEROUS FREEDOM."

Trey followed Anthony out the door and into the parking lot. Trey shut the door behind them as Anthony motioned for him to follow. They walked a good way's away from the door and stopped in front of a plain looking car. Anthony turned and handed Trey a set of keys.

"I'm assuming the Hummer is yours, so this is going to be a bit of a difference," Anthony told him. Trey look longingly at his beautiful Hummer parked at the opposite end of the parking lot.

"I brought y'all a 2014 Camry. It's one of the most common cars, so it will help y'all to blend in when you're traveling. The windows are tinted pretty dark too, so y'all should be straight with this ride. You know anything about cars?" Anthony asked, grilling Trey.

"I know enough," Trey shot back defensively.

"I checked out everything under the hood myself, so there shouldn't be any issues anyway. There's a jack and jumper cables in the trunk with the spare and a few tools you may need... extra oil... shit like that. Whenever you get where you're going, I can see about getting a truck and another motorcycle for Blaze. I know she's going to damn near be having withdrawals from not being able to ride," Anthony said, looking back in the direction of the room they just left.

"That's not the real reason I brought you out here, though," Anthony said, while opening the back door of the car to retrieve all the things he brought for Blaze.

"You and I need to talk man to man about all this," Anthony told him. Trey simply nodded his head for Anthony to continue.

"That is my daughter in there... my baby girl. I need to know you are in this for real and not just because she uhhh... well, because she... you know what I'm trying to say. She makes you feel good physically and all that bullshit," Anthony said, visibly flustered at the mere mention of his daughter having sex. Trey wanted to laugh out loud at the fact that big, bad, tough Anthony couldn't even verbalize the fact of his daughter being intimate with someone, but he figured it would be best if he didn't.

"I really do love your daughter. I know it literally happened in the blink of an eye, but that doesn't make it any less real. I sacrificed the career I spent my whole life building in order to keep her safe. I'm in it too. At this point, if we got caught, we would probably get the same amount of prison time," Trey told him.

"That's good to hear, but I also know you've never lived your life on the other side of the law, and Blaze practically grew up in it. Life on the run is rough. It can get real savage when push comes to shove. You're going to have to do what's necessary to survive and stay out of cuffs... the both of you. There may be times you have to do things that are against everything you believe in, but it's too late for second guessing now. Can you promise you'll handle business if need be?" Anthony asked. His eyes bore a hole through Trey as he stood waiting for the proper response.

"I will always do what needs to be done—no matter what—to keep us out of harm's way. No matter how gritty it gets, I'll protect Egypt," Trey said. Anthony looked at him skeptically, and Trey put up his right hand with two fingers held up.

"Scout's honor!" he said jokingly.

"You telling me my daughter really got a thing for your corny ass?"

Both of them laughed as Trey grabbed the bags filled with Blaze's things. Anthony closed the trunk, and they made their way back to the hotel room. Trey glanced toward the other end of the parking lot again and gazed upon his beautiful Hummer. Sadness crept over him because he knew it was as good as gone. His vehicle was too noticeable, so that meant it was a no-go. He looked at Blaze who was peeping out the window, trying to see what was taking them so long. Immediately, Trey's sadness left him, and he felt silly. He mentally blew a kiss goodbye at his favorite toy and followed Anthony inside to make some plans.

CHAPTER 24
BLAZE

"THE BEGINNING OF THE UNKNOWN IS FULL OF UNCERTAINTY."

Blaze opened the door for her father and Trey as they brought in a few bags with some of her things in them. Trey set down the bags he had on the bed. Blaze noticed a few things hanging out of the bags with tags on them.

"I had to get everything brand new, baby girl. Your crib is already being watched... your old crib," Anthony said. He had an empty suitcase he set on the bed.

"I just got a bunch of different clothes so you could try things on and pick out what you like," Anthony added while noticing Blaze's somber expression.

"Thanks, Pops. I don't know what I would do without you," Blaze said as she walked over to give her father a hug.

"All your primpy stuff is in one of these bags," Anthony told his daughter. She burst out in laughter while Trey and Anthony looked at each other.

"Do you mean my toiletries?" she asked.

"Oh yeah, yeah. That's what I was talking about, but everything that you'll need is in there. I did the best I could," he said while handing Blaze an envelope. She peeked inside, and there was a lot of money in it.

"Now y'all are going to have to stay here for a while. Let me explain before you look at me like that. I need to try to draw the FEDs in a different direction. I'll take the Hummer and clean it up... get the Kings to detail it from head to toe, then the chase starts. I'm going to head north and make sure I stop at a bank and a couple gas stations. They will have those places flagged, watching for you both and that Hummer... maybe buy some food and things with a bank card of yours. When I get far enough away, I'll call. Always be waiting and ready for that call because when it comes, y'all need to haul ass. You always have to be prepared to pack up and go in a matter of minutes, but baby girl already knows that," Anthony told them.

"I don't know about waiting here, Pops. We're only a couple of hours away from Leather and Lace, and it's not like it's vacant here. Other people staying here could recognize us or something from the news," Blaze said as she walked toward the window and peeped out at the parking lot.

"Nothing has come out yet on the news because they don't want anyone knowing this chick who runs shit escaped from their custody because of a rogue agent," Anthony told her, trying to make some of her anxiety dissipate.

"Okay. Well, hurry. I'll actually feel better if we're moving and not sittin' ducks," Blaze added on. Anthony hugged Blaze and kissed her on the forehead. He stepped to Trey with absolute seriousness in his expression.

"Remember what I said, son," he said as he pulled Trey in for a hug as well. Blaze watched her father walk out the door and eventually pull off in Trey's Hummer. Blaze didn't know what would happen, but she had ill feelings about everything at this point.

CHAPTER 25
ROXY

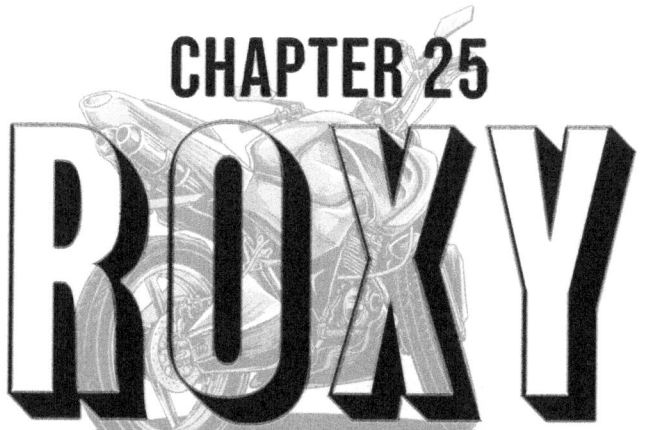

"YOU KNOW THE SAD THING ABOUT BETRAYAL? IT NEVER COMES FROM THE ENEMY."

"Latoya Simmons!" a voice yelled loudly. Roxy blinked her eyes open and sat up on her bed. Calling it a bed would actually be generous. It was closer to thick cardboard by the way that her back was feeling. She got up and walked over to the door, sticking her hands through the slot to get handcuffed. The CO put them on a little tight, but there was no use complaining. Roxy was damn near used to it by now. She pulled her hands back into her cell and took a few steps back.

"Pop seventeen!" the guard yelled again. Roxy's door slid open, and the guard came in, bending down to shackle her feet.

"What's this about? Is all this really necessary?" Roxy asked him.

"Move, inmate. You'll find out when you get there," he told her with an attitude.

"Where is *there*?" Roxy asked. The guard pushed her, causing her to slightly trip over her shackled feet. She knew her limits and knew not to ask any more questions. It had been three weeks since the raid on Leather and Lace. The FEDs had taken both Roxy and Laila into custody. She hadn't seen Laila nor had she heard anything from anyone on the outside. She knew no one's phone number by heart. They might as well had thrown her in a box with no windows or anything.

Roxy shuffled down the hall with the guard through a set of double doors. When they finally got to their destination, they stopped in front of a room with a small window. She glanced inside and saw a table with three chairs. It looked just like the interrogation rooms she had seen in the past.

"You've got special visitation... have fun," the guard said with a sinister grin on his face. Roxy's heart immediately dropped into her stomach. The CO took her into the room and took her handcuffs off, only to make her sit down and cuff her to the table. Roxy was left alone for what seemed like forever before two men in suits finally entered the room. They sat down opposite Roxy and stared for a moment. She leaned back in her chair, preparing for what she was about to hear.

"Ms. Simmons... you've been here in for a few weeks and could possibly be facing murder charges... at the very least, accessory after the fact. Did you happen to notice who you don't see here with you behind these bars?" the man asked. Roxy gave him a side eye and said nothing.

"Your boss, Blaze... that's who. You're in here and locked up like an animal. You can't shower when you want. You can't eat what you want or when you want, all while she's still out there roaming free. She is going to let you take the fall for something she did a long time ago," he said, taunting her.

"I call bullshit," Roxy said calmly while looking back and forth between the men. The one who was asking the questions gave a short nod to the other. He casually stood up and walked across the room to cut the power to the camera that was high in the corner.

Suddenly, Roxy felt a bicep around her neck. The man who had turned off the camera had come from behind and started choking her. Roxy was grabbing and scratching at his arm, but he only tightened his grip.

"Now look..." the man continued while calmly leaning back in his chair.

"...You and I both know you had nothing to do with this cold case murder. You didn't even know Egypt back then, but if you don't help us to locate her and Deontre Daniels, I will use all my power and connections to make sure you stay back here for a long fucking time. Even when they do decide to finally let you out, I will jam your kids so far into the system you'll never find them, let alone get them back," he said with a completely different tone.

"And I may even get a couple of my extra friendly COs to pay you some nightly visits. They are going to tear that lil' pussy apart, and you'll be begging to write statements on everybody when we're done with you," the man said. He gave his partner another small nod, and the man released Roxy from her chokehold. She coughed, sputtered, and gasped for air, having been only moments from passing out.

"You know what? Fuck you, man!" Roxy yelled, getting emotional at the mention of her children and the thought of the already hands-on COs actually getting permission to come in and rape her every night.

"I don't know where either of them are. The deal a few months ago was that if I lead you to Blaze, you would clean my record up a little bit, help me get my kids back, and put me in witness protection afterward. It's not my fault y'all lost her once you had her. I'm telling you the truth. I don't know anything.

This shit ain't right," Roxy said through watery eyes while still rubbing her neck.

"Do I look like I give a fuck what you think is or isn't right? If you don't know anything, you better come up with a way to find out... or smoke her out of her hiding place, or you're done, bitch. And you can save the tears for someone who gives a fuck because I don't know you from a can of paint, and I don't give two raggedy fucks about those bastard kids of yours or what happens to them. I'm trying to save my career and cover my own ass, and I will bulldoze your pretty ass to do it," the man told her. Roxy sat deathly still, letting her tears fall silently. She was stuck between a rock and a hard place, and she felt that she had no choice.

"I'll do it," she managed to say.

"Smart choice," the man said to her. He stood up over her and then squatted down in front of her. The man reached between her legs and started stroking her pussy through her jail house jumpsuit. Roxy tensed up, wanting to fight back but knowing she would lose with one hand still being cuffed to the table.

"If you try to fuck me over, sweet cheeks, I'll fuck you back even harder," the man said menacingly. He stopped suddenly, drew back his fist, and punched Roxy in the jaw.

"What was that for?" his partner asked.

"Bored, I guess," the man said before he started to laugh. Roxy kept her head turned away from him, not knowing what was coming next. The man sat back down across the table from Roxy and fixed his clothes.

"I'm Agent Taylor... remember my name, bitch," he said while signaling his partner again. The man restored power to the camera, and Roxy looked up to see the red, record light turn back on.

"I'm sorry you couldn't be of more assistance to us, Ms. Simmons, but we'll be in touch," the investigator said. He had changed the tone of his voice back from menacing to professional for the camera. Roxy stayed silent as they stood up to leave the room. Dangerous or not, she would do what she needed to do to get her children back. If that meant sacrificing Blaze and Trey, then so be it.

CHAPTER 26
BLACK

"NO LASTING RELATIONSHIP IS FOUNDED UPON BETRAYAL, LUST, AND TREACHERY."

Black walked through the living room of Laila's house and peeked out the window. It was almost one in the morning, and if he was going to do this, he had to do it now.

"Hurry up, Laila! Damn!" he yelled down the hall. Black made sure he had his gun and the key to Blaze's place that he secretly made. He turned around and saw Laila coming down the hall, looking mean as ever.

"I was fixing my makeup, nigga. Don't yell at me, and don't rush me either. Don't forget that this is my house. You haven't paid not nan mothafuckin' bill in here the whole month you've been here... ain't bought a damn Hot Pocket or pack of Kool-Aid to bring up in this bitch... nothing!" she spat at him while grabbing her vest from the couch.

"You don't be talking any of that rah-rah shit when I'm beating that pussy up, now do you?" Black asked her while sneering. He had been shacking up with Laila ever since the raid at Blaze's bar, but they were already sick of each other. The only reason he stayed was because he felt his place was being watched, and he didn't know anyone else that he halfway trusted to stay with. He tried calling Anthony, but no one had seen or heard from him in weeks. If it wasn't for the amazing, toe-curling sex he and Laila had on a daily basis, he would have been gone. It was crazy how, in a matter of weeks, they had gone from being crazy about each other to arguing all the time. There was clearly only physical attraction between the two.

Laila rolled her eyes at him while throwing on her book bag.

"How are we supposed to be getting into Blaze's place, anyway? I'm not doing no stupid shit. I'm not busting no windows or helping kick down a door, so what's the plan?" she asked.

"We're not breaking in anywhere. I have a key, so we good," Black replied while walking toward the door.

"Why the hell do you still have a key to get in... make me bust you in yo' shit! I swear!" Laila threatened.

"I know good and gahdamn well you don't call yourself being jealous... ask too many questions anyway, man. Damn. Just shut the fuck up sometimes and follow the leader. Daddy got this," Black said while tapping his foot impatiently.

"Stupid bitch," he added under his breath.

"Come again? Say what?" she asked, daring him to repeat himself. Black rolled his eyes, knowing it was best to keep his comments to himself until they handled business.

"That's what the fuck I thought. Bring yo' Black ass on. Let's go, nigga," Laila said before taking one last look at herself in her reflective phone case. Laila and Black both jumped on to their motorcycles and sped off toward Blaze's place.

CHAPTER 27
ANGEL

"REVENGE IS A CONFESSION OF PAIN... OR A MEANS OF PAIN RELIEF."

Angel had been staying in a hotel off the interstate for a while now. All her attempts to contact Trey failed. She had no idea what was going on with the case, but at this point, it didn't matter. The only thing Angel cared about now was getting revenge against the woman who had killed her father.

Angel unlocked her phone and went to compose a text message...

Angel: ?????????

She sat waiting for about ten minutes for a response. Going weeks without answers was about to drive her crazy. She had to find out something today. Angel knew she couldn't stay at the hotel forever, living in limbo. All of a sudden, Angel's ringing phone interrupted her thoughts. She looked down at her screen and quickly picked up.

"Hello?" she answered anxiously.

"Do you know what time it is?" a voice whispered. Agent Taylor was beyond aggravated by his sleep being disrupted.

"Yeah. Yeah. Fuck what you talking about. I haven't heard

from your partner in weeks. What am I supposed to do now? Trey was quarterbacking this whole thing, and now I'm just here, twisting in the wind and twiddling my thumbs," she said, disregarding his question. Angel honestly hadn't been paying attention to what time it was when she called him. She just knew she needed answers, and it was now or never.

"Have you been under a rock for the past three and a half weeks? Trey isn't even an agent anymore. He's not on our side anymore. He's on theirs... or I should say *hers*. He helped Blaze escape once we finally caught her, and on top of that, we didn't even find the murder weapon," Agent Taylor told her.

"First of all, ain't no our side. I don't care how bad I want that bitch. I will never side with the police. I'm not on *your* side. Let's get that straight. We just have a common goal... no more, no less," Angel told him. The FEDs didn't know it, but Angel's plan was never to figure out the truth and then turn Blaze and her family over to the FEDs. She wanted to confirm what she pretty much knew already and then kill them all, one by one.

"Well it's a no go until we figure out without a shadow of a doubt if Blaze killed the man or not and if her father ordered it —" Taylor continued. Angel hung up the phone while Agent Taylor was still speaking. She had one more card to play. She decided she would break into Blaze's house to look for the murder weapon. If it wasn't at the club, then it had to be at Blaze's crib. If she could find that final piece to the puzzle, she could take out everyone involved, guilt free.

Angel hopped up and put on her riding boots. On her way out the door, she grabbed her leather gloves and her Nubian Riders vest. Before the sun came up, Angel was going to Blaze's old place to find out the truth for herself, one way or another.

CHAPTER 28
LAILA

"DESPERATE TIMES CALL FOR DESPERATE MEASURES."

Laila and Black made it to Blaze's place quickly and were still arguing as they made their way through the door.

"...because it's got nothing to do with jealousy. You shouldn't have a key to her place, period, especially now. I'm trying to look out for your dumbass, and you can't even see it," Laila said as she stepped inside behind Black.

"You, of all people, should be glad I had the key. If I didn't, it would have been your slim-thick ass, crawling through a window while trying to dodge shards of broken glass, so shut the fuck up and come on," Black told her. Once inside, the two of them looked around for a moment.

"Immaculately clean, as always," Black said as he admired the way nothing was out of place. Laila glared at him and slapped him on the back of the head.

"My place would be this clean too, if I wasn't having to pick up after your grown messy ass," she whispered.

"Not now, Laila. You really are touched in the head. Shit!" Black replied.

"Just go through everything. Look for any papers or anything that looks official... or maybe like a file with my name on it," Black commanded her. Laila was about to head toward Blaze's bedroom when Black grabbed her arm. She whipped around, ready to argue again, but he gave her a fierce look.

"Chill out. I was just going to say if you happen to see a gold torque wrench laying around, grab it," he added. Laila looked at him with complete confusion all over her face.

"Black, what the hell is a torque wrench?" she almost yelled.

"You're a member of a well-known motorcycle gang, constantly riding, and been doing all that for years. How the fuck you don't know what the fuck a torque—? You know what? Never mind. Just go," Black told her. Laila turned on the flashlight from her phone and headed toward Blaze's master bedroom.

When she walked in, she saw that it was just as she had remembered it. Laila flashed back in her mind to before Blaze had the renovations done in the club to add the changing rooms and mirrors and couches. The two of them would blast music from her stereo and dance around while they got ready to turn up. Laila went over to Blaze's dresser and saw some of their pictures still sitting up in frames. She picked up the largest one. Laila and Blaze were at her father's house, about to jump in the pool. Laila's hair wasn't even long enough for her trademark ponytail yet. She just had a head full of microbraids. Neither Laila nor Blaze even had tattoos in the picture. It was taken before there was such a thing as the Nubian Riders, before they were president and vice-president of anything, and before Laila had fucked up her friendship with Blaze by opening her legs to the wrong man.

Standing there, Laila's eyes filled up with tears. Fucking

someone's man had never been a big deal for Laila, but she never thought she would allow herself to hurt her best friend the way she had. There had to be a way to make it right. Laila felt she needed Blaze back.

Taking her book bag off, she was about to put the picture in it when she noticed something pale sticking out of Blaze's top drawer. Laila glanced at the bedroom door and paused, making sure she didn't hear Black coming down the hall. When she was sure that it was all clear, she slowly pulled the drawer open. Laila pushed back some of Blaze's panties and saw four manila folders. She picked them up and shined her light on them. Egypt Johnson, Anthony Johnson, and Kareem White, each had their own file. The fourth folder said Cold Case 11415. Laila knew this had to be what Black had come there for, but something in her gut was telling her this wasn't right. Something was up with Black, and she felt it from the moment he mentioned the plan to come there.

Laila held her breath, making sure she could still hear Black in the other room. When she did, she started taking papers from the folders, folding them, and tossing them into her bag. Stepping to Blaze's closet, she figured she would hide the folders there just in case Black thought to glance in the room and check behind her.

"Aye," Black whispered from the door. Laila nearly jumped out of her skin when she heard his voice, but the darkness in the room masked her startled expression.

"Did you find anything?" he asked, taking a step inside the room.

"Nah. I just saw a couple pair of her Moschino tops I always wanted. I figured she ain't coming back for them, and it would be a shame to let them go to waste so—"

Laila was interrupted by a shattering sound that came from the living room. Laila and Black looked at one another and nodded. Laila stuffed another top in her bag to cover up the papers she was hiding, and both she and Black pulled their heat from their vests. Making their way toward the noise, Black motioned for Laila to stop. Laila strained her eyes in the darkness and then walked over and cut the lights on.

"Uh uh. I knew I recognized this bitch. The darkness can't even cover up those loud ass, ugly ass highlights."

"What the hell are y'all doing here? I cased this place, and I didn't see anybody come in," Angel said.

"We used a key, bi—"

"Shut up, Black," Laila said. She took her book bag and vest off and set them on the couch.

"I've been waiting to beat this scandalous bitch's ass for a long time now, and I heard through the grapevine she was working for the FEDs against the Nubian Riders," Laila said aloud.

"Even if she does deserve to get her ass beat, now is not the time, and this most definitely ain't the place for it," Black cut in. He knew Laila and could tell when she was about to whoop some ass.

"Another time, bae. Another—"

Whop! It was too late. Laila picked up a candle and threw it at Angel. Angel ducked, and the candle crashed, but by the time she stood back up, Laila was on top of her.

"Y'all trippin'! What the fuck?" Black yelled. Laila was landing every single one of her jabs. Angel grabbed Laila by her ponytail and gripped it tightly. Angel slung Laila to the ground and tried to pin her there with her knees to take control, but

Laila had been in too many fights to allow herself to be pinned on the ground.

Laila got her leg from under Angel while wrapping it around Angel's small waist. When Angel was distracted by the move, Laila head-butted her and pushed her off. Black wanted to protest because of the danger of them being there in the first place. He needed to break the girls up, but his growing erection from watching Laila whoop Angel's ass stopped him in his tracks and caused him to hold his tongue.

Laila lunged at Angel, breaking the glass coffee table. There was a thunderous crash, and Black knew it was definitely time for them to go. He rushed over, stepping through the glass to grab Laila and go but not before Laila had already damn-near broken Angel's jaw.

"I'm good! Get off me, nigga!" Laila shouted. She ran to grab her vest and book bag as Angel laid moaning in the floor. When she reached the door, Black grabbed her and pulled her in close, sticking his long tongue down her throat. Laila, hype from the adrenaline of the fight, reached up to grab Black by the back of the neck, kissing him deeper. Laila broke the kiss first. She drew back and slapped the taste out Black's mouth. He glared at her with a hunger in his eyes. Black pushed Laila against the wall, pinning her there, as he reached up underneath her shirt and began gently playing with her nipple.

Suddenly, they stopped at the sound of sirens in the distance. One of Blaze's neighbors must have called the police because of the commotion from the fight.

"We'll finish this at home," Black told her while planting one more kiss on her lips. They grabbed their things, and with one last glance at Angel, who was still lying in the same spot beaten and bruised, they disappeared into the night.

CHAPTER 29
ROXY

"GOTTA DO WHAT YOU GOTTA DO."

Roxy was so glad this day had finally come. She walked down the pavement with her personal items in hand to the final gate of the jail. She stood there while the buzzer sounded, and the fence slid sideways. Roxy couldn't get away from that disgusting place quick enough. Those repulsive women were something she did not want to get used to. Part of her wanted to run out of those gates, but there was no point. She strained her eyes in the sun to peep out the parking lot when she saw a white tinted Grand Marquis. She looked around first and then quickly made her way to the car. She opened the door and sat inside, slamming it shut.

"Could you be more obvious?" she asked while looking at the driver. Agent Taylor looked back at her, smirking.

"Get me out of here. Everything about you is screaming cop right now. Damn," she added.

"You worry too much. You have something for me?" he asked.

"You have something for *me*?" Roxy asked, answering his

question with a question. He reached in his back seat and produced a plain white paper bag.

"Five Guys, double with everything on it, bacon included. There's a Fanta on the floor. Now, what do you have for me?" Agent Taylor asked again. Roxy ignored him while she took her burger out of the back and took a huge bite.

"Give me a couple days," she said with a mouthful of food. She was grubbing like she hadn't eaten in months.

"Do not play games with me, Toya. I'm serious! You have three days to start bringing me useful information, or I will throw your lil' cute ass back in a cell so fast and... well, you remember the first talk we ever had."

Agent Taylor paused and looked at Roxy from head to toe, sending an unwelcomed shiver through her body.

"Just get me what I need to find Blaze," he told her.

"Whatever, man. I've got it," she said while still stuffing her face.

"Just get me to my crib. I'm in need of a hot shower and a long ride on my bike... wind slapping my cheeks... yeah. That's what I need."

Roxy waited until she got to her apartment before checking her phone. She didn't want any unnecessary questions from Agent Taylor. She went to missed calls and saw that she had more than several from a number she didn't recognize. She double checked that her front door was locked and sat down at her dining room table as she called the number back. It rang for a long time before someone actually picked up, but the person didn't say anything.

"Hello?" Roxy said into her phone, making sure it had really connected the call.

"Baby girl, how are you? I was blowing your phone up until I heard they had you hemmed up in the county. Are you good?" asked that familiar deep booming voice.

"Anthony! I'm so glad to hear from you. I haven't heard anything in weeks. I'm good though. The FEDs got me on some bullshit fine that was overdue and gave me a lil' bullshit thirty days. Of course, they tried to drill me for info, threatening me and what not, but I wasn't going for it," Roxy told him, making sure to sound confident and ease any suspicions he may have had. Now that she thought about it, the fact that she hadn't heard from anyone made sense. When the word got out that she had been hemmed up, members of both clubs probably suspected she would flip to save her own ass.

"I know you, Rox. I didn't think for a second you would betray your family like that," Anthony replied, but she only half believed him.

"I'm glad you're out and everything though because I need your help, and you're the only one left we trust," he said.

"Yeah. Sure. Anything for you. What do you need, Ant?"

"I'm handling some business out of town. Blaze needs some help with the little things… just getting food and stuff like that. She needs to stay out of sight as much as possible until I finish handling this business. Can you do that for us?"

"Absolutely, Ant. That's no problem. I'll be glad to do it. It will be nice to see Blaze, too. I haven't seen her in about a month," Roxy told him.

"Okay. I'll call you back soon so that we can meet in person, and I can give you all the details. I don't trust the phone shit being that we're fucking with the FEDs. Matter of fact, I'll have a new cell phone for you when we meet," he told her.

Just like that, Anthony hung up without saying bye. Roxy looked down at the phone, thinking at first she had lost signal. Anthony had probably thought about the fact that someone could be listening to their calls already, so he had hung up. Roxy had to make sure she acted completely normal around him so he wouldn't be even more suspicious than he already was.

CHAPTER 30
BLAZE

"NOTHING WORSE THAN THE PERFECT SITUATION WITH BAD TIMING."

Blaze and Trey had been at the dingy motel for several weeks now awaiting her father's call saying that the coast was clear. The two of them were getting restless. The only thing they could do to pass the time was eat, watch TV, and make love. This particular day, none of those activities were working out. Blaze had been irritable since she woke up because she wasn't feeling well. She had been cooped up in the bathroom for almost an hour.

"Bae, you okay?" she heard Trey ask from the door.

"I'm good. I'll be out in a minute. I think that leftover Chinese food I had last night was spoiled or something!" she yelled back while still kneeling in front of the bowl.

"Okay... holla if you need me," he replied. Blaze heard him turn on the TV, and she knew now was her only chance. The noise from the TV would be the perfect cover. Reaching into her bra, she pulled out a pregnancy test from her cleavage. Blaze peeled off the wrapping as quietly as she could. Getting off her knees, she pulled down her clothes to take the test.

"Are you okay for a minute, baby? I've got to use the bathroom real quick!" Trey hollered at her.

"Okay. Just give my like five more minutes!" she yelled back. Blaze capped the test and set it on the floor. Sitting there waiting for the results, her mind was spinning. The two of them had been so stupid. From the first time they made love, neither one of them had even brought up the topic of using a condom. What the hell were they going to do if the test was positive? How could they be on the run with her carrying a child? How would she be able to go to a doctor without being arrested? Blaze's questions were endless.

What seemed like more than three minutes passed, and Blaze looked down. She immediately grabbed the burner phone from the bathroom counter to text Roxy.

Blaze: 911 I need you

CHAPTER 31
LAILA

"YOU COULD BE SLEEPING NEXT TO THE DEVIL AND NOT EVEN KNOW IT."

Laila laid on Black's chest, listening to his heartbeat until she was sure he was in a deep sleep. She may have gotten turned on after beating Angel's ass, but that didn't make her forget the reason they had been there in the first place. Black had been looking for something he needed to destroy, and the fact that he wouldn't give Laila all the details meant he was hiding something.

She eased herself from the bed slowly so as not to wake him, and she went to grab her bag from the living room. Tiptoeing to her bathroom with the papers from the files at Blaze's crib, she shut the door, locked it, and cut on the shower. She decided to pick up the file with Black's name on it first, and nothing could have prepared her for what she was about to read...

United States Department of Justice
Federal Bureau of Investigation
Date of transcription: June 10, 2018:

Kareem White was interviewed by properly identified Special Agents of the Federal Bureau of Investigation. White provided the following information about case file 11415 involving the charge of First-Degree Murder of Dominic Ruiz against prime suspect, Egypt Johnson:

In May of 2001, Egypt was informed by an inside source that there was a hit out on her father, Anthony Johnson. She told her father about the greenlight, and his plan was to be diplomatic with the leader of Dominican crew, Dominic Ruiz. In fear for her father's life, Egypt constructed a plan to murder Ruiz before he could bring harm to Anthony.

On July 1, 2002, Egypt Johnson attended a nightclub that Ruiz frequented. She persuaded Ruiz into taking her to his home. Egypt Johnson had sexual relations with victim, Ruiz. As the victim slept, Egypt Johnson bludgeoned his head with a golden torque wrench. When Ruiz did not immediately die, Egypt Johnson tied him to his bedpost and set the house on fire, originating from the bedroom, in order to finish the task and eliminate all traces of her DNA in the house and on Ruiz's person.

Informant statement: {She (Egypt Johnson) called me (Kareem White), her fiancé at the time, to confide in me about what she had done. She and I had sex following that. Afterward, she convinced me to hide the torque wrench for her at her establishment, Leather and Lace. I placed the weapon inside the locker of Latoya Simmons who, at that time, had no knowledge of the weapon or any events surrounding its placement with her property.}

In accordance with Mr. White's full cooperation with the Federal Bureau of Investigation, he will receive immunity from any and all charges related to cold case file 11415 and the indictment of Egypt Johnson. Enclosed for your information is the FBI File Fact Sheet, case files on Anthony Johnson, a.k.a Hulk, Egypt Johnson, a.k.a Blaze, and cooperating informant Kareem White, a.k.a Black.
Signed,
Deputy Director Chief

Laila was practically trembling after what she had just read. She couldn't believe she had been left in the dark about this. After all these years, she realized Anthony gave Blaze her nickname because that crazy bitch had burned someone alive, and not only that, but Black, the man who she had been lying next to at night, helped her.

The craziest part was that Laila wasn't even that upset to find out that her former best friend was a murderer. She was livid that she had been associating herself with a snitch. Laila had long since come to terms with the fact that she was a fucked up individual for sleeping with the man that her best friend used to be in love with, but something that was drilled into her for as long as she could remember was that snitches ended up in ditches.

Laila turned off the shower and left the bathroom, returning the papers to their place in her bag. She walked back down the hall and glanced in her bedroom where Black was sleeping peacefully. Laila stepped into her closet with retribution on her mind, when she heard Black to stir.

"Baby! Where you at, girl? I'm recharged and ready for round two. Bring that juicy ass in here and hop on this dick!" Black yelled to her.

"Okay, bae. I'll be right there. I wanted to try something different with you!" Laila yelled while looking for her Nubian Riders vest in the dark. Black could hear her rummaging through the closet.

"Aww shit, now. What you trying to do to me? You breaking out some handcuffs or a whip... something freaky like that!" Black yelled.

"You'll see in juuuuust a second, bae. I'm about to blow your fucking mind!" Laila yelled. She grabbed her revolver and was putting the bullets in as quietly as she could.

"You ready for me to put this good pussy in ya life, Black?" Laila yelled as she finished loading her gun. She was met with silence.

"Black... baby!" she yelled. Again, she was met with silence. Laila rounded the corner with her revolver aimed at the bed, and she was met by Black with his pistol pointed right back at her.

"I guess you thought I was fucking stupid or something huh, bitch," Black said with a sinister smirk on his face. Laila had damn near dropped her revolver when she had turned the corner and came face to face with Black. How did he know she knew everything?

"I knew what you would probably do from the moment I caught you in Blaze's bedroom acting strange," Black said.

"You're a gahdamn rat, Black. How did you think things would end for you? Did you think you would give your statement to the FBI and then you would disappear into the witness protection program and live happily ever after? You were dead from the moment you wrote that statement on Blaze. If I don't kill you, somebody else from the Nubian Riders or the Kings will. My money is on Blaze and Anthony finding you, though," Laila said. At this point, she was gripping her gun so tightly that her fingers hurt.

"There's a flaw in your logic, Laila. If I just kill you right now, no one will ever even know I told," Black said with a smile.

"See, that's where you're wrong, nigga. The FBI agent, Trey... he switched sides, dummy. He knows everything, which means Blaze probably does too at this point."

Laila looked at Black and could practically see his heart sink down to his feet. His flinched, and both of them fired their guns.

Pow! Pow!

There was a loud yell and then silence as the smell of gun powder circulated in the room. A body hit the floor with a thud as cries of pain reverberated through the air.

CHAPTER 32
ROXY

"LIVING OFF THE GRID AND BEING AN OUTLAW BRINGS A DANGEROUS REALITY."

Roxy pulled up to the dingy motel where Blaze and Trey were staying. A few hours before, Roxy received a 911 text from Blaze. Judging by the content of the message, Roxy assumed it had something to do with the pregnancy test Blaze asked her to get the day before.

Roxy grabbed the food she bought for them and knocked on the door. When Blaze answered, she widened her eyes, looking crazy.

"Uhh... hey, girl. How are y'all?" Roxy said while stepping inside and looking at Blaze like she had lost her mind.

"Hey, girl! Me and Trey are good... nothing major at all going on today. We've just been chilling, watching old hood movies all day. Are you eating with us?" Blaze asked. Roxy watched her as her eyes continued to go crazy, widening and darting back and forth between Trey and the door. Suddenly, it clicked in Roxy's mind. Blaze hadn't told Trey anything about her suspicions that she was pregnant. Blaze was trying to signal Roxy not to say anything in front of Trey. Roxy laughed to herself and gave Blaze a hug and squeezed her, holding her extra tight to let her know that she understood.

"Trey, I'm going to borrow Blaze for a minute. It's just girl talk," Roxy told him.

"That's fine with me. I'm about to grub. Talk as long as y'all need to. Don't forget your hat and shades, baby," Trey added while opening up his plate of home cooked food from Roxy. When they got outside, tears immediately fell from Blaze's eyes.

"I'm confused! What's wrong?" Roxy asked, putting her arm around Blaze.

"Let's walk this way," Blaze said while looking back at the door to her and Trey's room. They stopped, and she turned to face Roxy with a somber look on her face.

"The pregnancy test was positive," Blaze told her while silent tears continued to fall.

"Damn... I don't know what to say, Blaze. I would say congratulations, but judging by your tears, this ain't a joyous occasion," Roxy said while looking into Blaze's eyes.

"I want nothing more than to settle down and start a family with the man I love, but I can't keep this baby, Roxy. Think about it. How are we going to keep running from the law while I'm as big as a house? When I give birth, how am I supposed to get a doctor or midwife to deliver? What about after the baby is born? This isn't going to be possible, Roxy," Blaze said while wiping the tears that were still falling.

"Baby girl, we're nowhere near the time for you to give birth yet. You've got a while before that happens. Plus, you won't be on the run forever. Your father is working his contacts to find a place for y'all to disappear to permanently. You know he's not going to let his one and only sit in prison for the rest of her life," Roxy told her.

"I hear you, and it sounds good, but you're not the one living this, Rox," Blaze replied while looking back toward their room door.

"Look... I haven't told anyone else this, but I'm trying to get my kids back. Once I do that, we could come settle with y'all, and I could help y'all with the baby. There's always a way," Roxy told her. Blaze hugged Roxy tight.

"Oh my God! I had no idea. That's great, Roxy. Are you sure you would leave with us? You would leave your life behind?"

"My kids are my life... and my best friend, of course. I would love to start a new chapter with y'all. Plus, I've got two kids... that's a lot of experience, girl. I've got you."

"I hear you. I'm still gonna think on it," she told her. All of a sudden, Roxy's phone started vibrating like crazy.

"I'll be in there. I'm just going to check this," Roxy said. She watched Blaze head back into the room and then pulled her phone out of her pocket. She had a few new text messages. She clicked on the envelope icon and swallowed hard when she started reading.

Agent Taylor: *You're running out of time*
Agent Taylor: *Don't forget our deal... need a location NOW!*

Roxy deleted the messages, not knowing what to do. She couldn't turn in the woman who had literally brought her out of the gutter and given her a chance at a new start. Blaze truly was like a sister to her. Roxy also couldn't put off helping Agent Taylor any longer because she would have to face losing her two children to the system forever. Out of nowhere, it hit her. She had the perfect plan to ensure that she got her children back, and Blaze and Trey would stay free. She looked back at her phone so she could send some messages.

. . .

Roxy: *Super 8 motel off highway 85, room 227, they left to eat, wait an hour, then go*

Roxy sent the message to Agent Taylor and then took off toward the room where Blaze and Trey were. She burst through the door, locking it behind her.

"I've got a friend on the inside who just gave me a tip. Someone out here recognized you guys. The FEDs are on their way. We've got to go *now!*" Roxy told them. Trey jumped up, knocking over the food he had and started zipping up the bags. Roxy ran to their car to open the trunk and started taking things from the room and throwing them in. They were ready to go in minutes.

"Go! I'll handle this!" Roxy told them as she shut the door, placing the room keys out of sight, under a nearby bush.

"Come with us... Please!" Blaze begged. Looking into her eyes, Roxy could tell Blaze was scared out of her mind and desperate for help after just confirming she was pregnant that morning. Roxy paused and thought about her own children. When she was in need, there had been no one at all to help her until Blaze had come along, and she owed the woman her life.

"Shit! Okay, baby girl," she agreed while putting on her helmet and starting her motorcycle. All three of them stood frozen as they heard sirens in the far distance. *I told those mothafuckas an hour. Taylor must have already had a tail on me,* Roxy thought to herself.

"Time to get the fuck out of here," Trey told them to break the trance that the sound of the sirens had put on them. Roxy quickly whipped her phone back out to shoot Anthony a text.

Roxy: *couldn't wait, shit went down, on the move!*

Roxy put her phone back, and it almost immediately started to vibrate, but she didn't have time to check it right then. She hauled ass on her motorcycle with Blaze and Trey right on her tail, heading in no specific direction except far away from that motel. Roxy had no idea what the future held, but she knew she now had a lot of people's fates in her hands.

Sneak peek of "In Love With An Outlaw Part Two"

CHAPTER 1
BLAZE

"JUST... RUN."

Blaze sat in the passenger seat of the Camry with her stomach twisted in knots. Mentally, she was in a completely different place. Less than an hour ago, she had been at the motel with Trey, trying to figure out how she was going to give him the news that she was pregnant. After Roxy arrived and told them they had to high-tail it out of there, Blaze felt like her life had been uprooted yet again. One second, she was discussing the future of her family and the possibility of bringing a new life into the world in a brand-new place. The next second, she was being brought back to a not so joyous reality by learning that the police were still hot on their trail. Blaze knew what the outlaw life was like because of her past, but after laying her eyes on that positive pregnancy test, her perspective changed almost in an instant.

"What's wrong, babe?" Trey asked as he glanced back and forth between Blaze and the road ahead.

"Nothing. I'm just on edge. That's all. Hearing the sirens back there and everything... I just feel like it was a close call this time... too close. I'm just shaken up a little bit," she told him while glancing in the rearview mirror.

"We're good. We got out in time, and there's no way they will find us right now. Hell, we don't even know where we're going, so there's no way we'll have cuffs waiting on us when we get there," Trey told her.

"Yeah. You're right. I just have this funny feeling in my gut that something is off with all of this, but it's probably nothing. It seems like they're fuckin' mind readers. Every move we make, they're right there. I don't know... Just keep driving until we need to stop for gas. We should head east toward SC," Blaze told him while reaching to pick up the burner cell.

"SC? You mean South Carolina? Why the hell would we go that country ass place?" Trey asked, continuing to glance at Blaze every so often with a genuinely confused expression on his face.

"Trey, we've got to start thinking long term. We can't be on the run forever. You can't see it now, but this shit will start to take a toll on you after a while; physically, mentally, and emotionally. If you and I don't eventually want to spend the rest of our lives behind bars, then we need an end game. We've got to get out the country," she said.

Blaze stared out the window at the highway and started to imagine what life could be like if she could rewind time to before she had done any of the dirt in her past. She and Trey could just start over with a clean slate and live what society would deem a normal life...

"Trey, hurry up! You've got to see this!" Blaze yelled. Trey came sprinting down the hall of their five-bedroom ocean front home and into the kitchen where Blaze was seated.

"What's wrong? Is it time? Do we need to get to the hospital?" asked an out of breath Trey. He walked over to the Vendome glass dining table

where Blaze was seated. Making his way around the table, a grin slowly spread across his face as he laid eyes on a very pregnant Blaze sitting next to their baby girl's highchair. She was in tears from laughter, and the baby girl was squealing with joy.

"You're supposed to eat that, not paint yourself with it, jellybean," Trey said as he lifted their daughter from her highchair. She was covered all over in bits of food and barbecue sauce.

"I literally looked away for five seconds, and this was what happened. That's real talent right there. Our girl is quick with her hands. She must get that from you," Blaze said while wiping the tears that had ensued from her laughter.

"You got jokes, huh? It's all good. It's my turn to clean her up this time anyway." Trey leaned down and gave Blaze a peck on the lips before he proceeded to walk back down the hall he had just come from. Blaze was about to get up from the table and assist in the cleaning a little, but suddenly, she felt a gut-wrenching pain that stopped her in her tracks and cried out.

"Trey! Trey! Baby, I think it really is time!" Blaze yelled at the top of her lungs. She sat back, expecting Trey to come running again, but she was met with silence. There was no response from him and not even the beautiful sound of the giggling baby girl. Slowly getting up from her seat, she made her way down the hall. Another pain shot through her belly, causing her to double over in agony.

"Trey, I know you hear me. Get the bags! We've got to go, now!" she yelled again, this time nearly in tears. Blaze rounded the corner and walked into the bathroom.

"Trey?" Blaze said quizzically, her voice echoing back at her in an unusually loud manner. She shut the bathroom door and turned on the lights, only to reveal that she was no longer in her home but on a cell block.

"What the —?"

"You're absolutely right, Blaze," Trey said, interrupting Blaze's daydream and causing her to jerk abruptly.

"We've gotten this far, so there's no turning back now. I know for damn sure I can't go to prison. Do you know what the fuck they'd do to a former Fed in there? A Black one at that? Hell no. Everything happens for a reason. We're meant to be together, and I don't give a fuck if we have to get new identities and all. We're going to be together," he said with authority and finality. Blaze grabbed Trey's free hand and squeezed it tightly. She knew now what she had to do to help them both survive. Using her other hand, Blaze went to the messages in their burner phone and proceeded to text her father.

Blaze: *we good... on the road*
Anthony: *direction?*
Blaze: *east*
Anthony: *K, I'll keep heading west with Hummer*
Blaze: *how is my club???*
Anthony: *suffering... police raid scared regulars... got my guys running it...with Laila*
Blaze: *need to hit the sky soon*
Anthony: *bet, I'll make it happen*

Blaze put the phone back in the center console, satisfied that her father was on top of things, and turned back to Trey.

"I've got a plan, I think," she said.

"I'm down for whatever, bae. What you got in mind?" Trey replied. Blaze started smiling from ear to ear once he said that.

"That's music to my ears because we've gotta be in this together. We've gotta head east because I know someone with a plane we can use. I was thinking that if you can use your connects to get us some new identities, we can get the fuck out of here real soon," Blaze told him anxiously.

"Okay. Once this heat that's on us from today dies down a little, I'll make some calls. I have an uhh... I have a person that can make some things happen for us," Trey said, quickly cutting his eyes over at Blaze.

"Do you completely trust him?"

"Yeah. I most definitely trust him. He owes me his life."

"That's perfect. I feel a little better about things. We just have to be smart and always watch each other's back. There's no turning back. We're in this—"

"Forever," Trey said, completing her sentence for her. Trey picked her hand up and kissed the back of it as they interlocked their fingers. Blaze paused, looked at Trey, and then started laughing while thinking of what he'd just said.

"Bae, I think we've gotten corny as hell. *Together forever?* That's some fairy tale shit. This is real life. We gotta keep from gettin' locked up first before we start talkin' about some happily ever after shit."

Trey couldn't do anything but laugh as well.

"Whatever. Cliché or not, that's how a nigga feel." Trey glanced up, checking the rearview mirror and then checked the side view as well.

"Roxy still back there?" Trey asked. Blaze turned back and saw Roxy's black and white Kawasaki ZZR 1400 motorcycle dipping between other cars. Watching it longingly for a few minutes, she thought about the rush she used to get when she was speeding down the road with the wind whipping through her hair. It had been a long time since she was able to feel the freedom of being on her own motorcycle. As quickly as she and Trey's romance had blossomed and then turned them into outlaws, it felt like a lifetime ago that she was carefree, running her bar, and making money with her bike club, the Nubian Riders.

"Blaze?" Trey asked, interrupting her thoughts yet again.

"Oh yeah. My bad. Yeah. She's still back there. She'll see us when we decide to stop," Blaze told him. Blaze faced forward, turned on the radio, and allowed the sounds of Kendrick Lamar to drown out her own invasive thoughts of what her life used to be and how things were never going to be the same.

CHAPTER 2
LAILA

"STICK TO THE STORY."

There was a silence in the room where Laila stood with a vacant look in her eye. She had always been a fighter, but she had never killed anyone before. There wasn't much time to think about if she was going to make it out of this situation. There was no way the neighbors hadn't heard the gunshot and the scream, so the police would be there before she knew it. Laila figured she would turn into the beaten and battered girlfriend so she could play the self-defense card once the authorities arrived. She had to stage it well if it was going to be believable and keep her from getting locked up.

Reaching over to the dresser to pick up the first thing she saw, which happened to be one of Black's bike show trophies, she prepared herself for the pain that would follow from bashing her own head in.

Just do it, bitch. You damn sure ain't built for prison, Laila thought, hyping herself up to hit herself over the head. Laila gritted her teeth and closed her eyes while raising the trophy when she heard a faint moan come from the floor. She paused mid-strike, too afraid to say anything at first. She looked down at the seemingly lifeless body that she had been ignoring for the past few minutes, only to see it slightly reanimate. Black was still alive but barely, from the sound of it. Through his harsh shallow breathing, he spoke.

"9-1-1," Black managed to get out in a whisper. Laila stood frozen for a moment and grabbed Black's phone from the nightstand. She dialed 9-1-1 and placed the phone on the floor next to him.

"9-1-1, what's your emergency?" she heard the operator say.

"Hello?" the operator repeated when Black didn't respond. Laila looked at Black with panic in her eyes until he managed to whisper her address well enough for the dispatcher to hear. As soon as there was confirmation that the police and an ambulance was in route, Laila hung the phone up. Her initial shock from the whole situation had worn off, and she was now in survival mode. She bent down over Black and spoke with a different type of ferocity in her tone.

"If you snitch on me to the police, I will come back and finish you," Laila threatened. She stood up and jammed her foot into Black's stomach where the bullet wound was. He cried out in pain, sounding like a wild animal.

"Black, focus on my voice," Laila started, speaking as quickly as possible. Her voice sounded stern and serious, but on the inside, she was a nervous wreck, and her heart was about to jump out of her chest.

"I was here earlier. I left to go to the club, and shortly after, someone broke in and shot you. That's the story you need to tell. I'll send your stuff to your old apartment, but you may want to get the hell out of town as soon as you're able to. If you even dream about coming for me when you're healed, you better wake the fuck up and check yourself. When everybody finds out what you did... how you're a thoroughbred snitch, especially Anthony, you're as good as dead," Laila finished as she removed her foot from his limp frame. Throwing on random clothes, Laila left her house, leaving Black lying on the floor and bleeding out. Laila hopped on her motorcycle and sped off toward Leather and Lace.

As soon as she pulled around the back of the club, she pulled out her cellphone and dialed Roxy's number. She tried four times to get Roxy on the phone, but she couldn't get an answer. Laila was really trying to solidify an alibi just in case Black was stupid enough to tell the cops what really went down.

Laila pulled out the spare key that she still had to the club and slipped in the back door. It was eerie being inside the club alone. Ever since Blaze disappeared, Laila was in charge. Blaze hadn't had the chance to vote her out of her position of Vice-President, but even with the title, barely anyone respected her once word got out about her fuckin' around with Black.

As if it wasn't hard enough to run an organization where no one wanted you as the leader, Laila never realized how much went into just keeping the bar up and running, let alone being in charge of all the Nubian Riders. Laila wasn't nearly as organized as Blaze nor was she used to the power and responsibility.

She only opened Leather and Lace Thursdays through Sundays, as opposed to when Blaze was there. Her friend opened the bar damn near every day because Leather and Lace had become a safe haven for the Nubian Riders and their brothers, the Kings, to let loose.

Laila really missed her best friend and wanted to do whatever she could to win her way back into Blaze's life. Laila knew she was dead wrong for even thinking about Black in a sexual way, let alone acting on those thoughts. When she sat reflecting on all the years she and Blaze had been tight, she wanted to slap herself for being so stupid. To add insult to injury, Black wasn't even worth it. He ended up being a dog ass snitch, and Laila hadn't even had the guts to finish the job after botching his murder attempt. The moment she'd heard Black take another breath, she should have bashed his head in with his own trophy right then and there instead of letting him live. Maybe if she went to Blaze with a plan to get rid of Black for good, she would accept that as an apology.

Laila decided that she would crash at the bar until the events from the night had blown over. She walked over to the bar with intentions of grabbing her personal bottle of Crown Royal and heading to the back office where the couch was. Before she could even get her hands on the liquor, her phone rang. She looked at her phone screen and it simply read *unavailable*. She looked at it hesitantly, but she decided to pick up.

"Hello?" Laila answered.

"May I speak with Ebony Jones?" the voice asked.

"Yeah. This is she," Laila said.

"This is Officer Odell with the Bell County Police Department. There was an incident at your residence," the officer said. Laila grew nervous, wondering if they were about to bring her in for questioning as a person of interest.

"Apparently, there was a break-in. A Mr. Kareem White was shot and injured. He gave a brief description of the perps before losing consciousness. The two men that broke in are still at large. You may want to stay with a friend or relative for the next few nights. At the moment, we're unclear as to what the motive behind this attack was, and these men could very well return," he said. A wave of relief washed over Laila once she knew Black stuck with the story.

"Oh my goodness! Is Kareem okay?" Laila asked, faking her concern.

"The paramedics said he's in critical condition. If I were you, I would want to be by my partner's side at the hospital as quickly as possible. We really don't know how things are going to go."

"Thank you so much, officer. I'm going to hop back on the highway to come see him," Laila said, making her voice sound shaky as if she was fighting back tears. *I deserve a gahdamn Oscar for this performance*, Laila thought to herself.

"Your apartment is still an active crime scene, so one of us will be in contact with you so we can bring you anything you may need from your place like clothes or any other personal effects."

"Okay. Thank you again, officer. I'll be looking for your call," Laila said before hanging up. She smirked, grabbed her Crown Royal, and took a huge swig before heading to the back office to catch some sleep.

Thanks for reading! I hope In Love With An Outlaw truly took you on a journey into the lives of these characters. Be sure to leave a review and let know me know what you think! The more the merrier because I do it for my readers.

Also, be sure to follow me on social media to get sneak peeks, exclusive offers, upcoming events where you can "meet the author", and don't be afraid to interact!

CONNECT WITH REIGN

Facebook: Reign Vance
Instagram: reignvance

"Writing isn't just a thing... it's my release. There's a little piece of me in all my characters... a lot of truth in all my stories."
-Patesha V.

Made in the USA
Columbia, SC
11 February 2022